MASON

FEDERAL PROTECTION AGENCY

BOOK ONE

BY EVIE RILEY

Mason

Federal Protection Agency

Book One

Copyright © 2022

Evie Riley

Second Edition

ISBN: 978-1-77357-664-0

Published by Naughty Nights Press LLC

Cover Art By Willsin Rowe

MASON

There is freedom in acceptance...

Agent Mason Wright works for Homeland Security focusing on crimes against children. He takes some much-needed time off to visit his brother, but his vacation unexpectedly turns into more work when he's assigned to create an impromptu task force to track down a corrupt cop on the run.

Detective Jarod Lopez is a new rookie on the police force. He keeps his head down and doesn't make waves, but that leaves him with little chance of his skills being put to good use. The coveted opportunity to join a recently developed task force drops in his lap and Jarod jumps at the opening.

Will desire ignite between the pair while they chase down the bad guy?

A sizzling, suspenseful romance, Mason is Book 1 in an exciting action adventure mm romance series.

Content Warning: Murder, Drugs, Abuse, Captivity, Crimes against children.

CHAPTER ONE

Mason

POSTTRAUMATIC STRESS DISORDER is a psychiatric disorder that may occur in people who have experienced or witnessed a traumatic event such as a natural disaster, a serious accident, a terrorist act, war/combat, or rape, or who have been threatened with death, sexual violence, or serious injury. Symptoms include: intrusive thoughts, nightmares, avoiding reminders of the event, memory loss, negative thoughts about self and the world, self-isolation, feeling distant, anger and irritability, reduced interest in favorite activities, hyper vigilance, difficulty concentrating, insomnia, vivid flashbacks, avoiding people, places and things related to the event, casting blame, difficulty feeling positive emotions, exaggerated startle response, and risky behaviors.

"What a bunch of bullshit," I said, and tossed my phone onto the dash of my rental truck.

The shrink I had hired to help me with my insomnia had just diagnosed me with PTSD and it was a load of shit. Just because I had some of the symptoms, didn't mean that was what was wrong with me.

I was able to function.

I was doing my job.

I just had some problems outside of it.

I was having a hard time sleeping, and when I did, I usually had nightmares. I was a bit on edge, but never in the field. I wasn't angry or lashing out at people. I wasn't having flashbacks or panic attacks. Sure, at times, I had a hard time sitting still. I got anxious sometimes at night but I would just go for a run with Koda and I was fine.

I didn't have PTSD.

Besides, I didn't even know where it would have come from. I was a federal agent with Homeland security. I specialized in crimes against children and, yes, I saw some horrific things, but nothing that the other Agents hadn't already seen.

Agents that had been on the job for twenty years were fine with the things we see, so how could that give me PTSD when it didn't with others?

The shrink was wrong. It was just that simple. Everyone struggled with sleeping from time to time.

And if I had to have a few drinks in the day to get through the night, then so what?

I never drank while on duty. It was always after work. I wasn't drinking an excessive amount, just enough to help me fall asleep when it had been a few days. I was coping and there was nothing wrong with it.

Koda whined beside me and I glanced over at him. Koda was my K9 partner, a beautiful German shepherd.

I loved this dog.

I didn't know what I would do without him.

I've always loved dogs and when the opportunity presented itself for me to be a K9 handler five years ago, I jumped at the chance. I've had Koda ever since he was an eight week old puppy, and I couldn't imagine not having him in my life.

My greatest fear is for Koda to be hurt in the field.

"You want to go and see Uncle Ro?" I asked the dog as I started to pet him. I was currently sitting in my rental truck out front of my older brother's house.

Roland, or Ro as I always called him, was a local cop. He was also ex-military and had been a cop in New York City before he moved out here. I was surprised when he decided to move to a smaller town like Gaithersburg, but it was his life and he was free to do with it as he wished.

He knew I was coming by, that I had taken some vacation days. He didn't know about the real troubles I'd been having with my sleep. I wasn't about to tell him and add to his own worries and stress.

Letting out yet another sigh, I removed my seatbelt and got out. I might as well get this over and done with. The second we opened the door and strolled inside, Koda ran right toward the kitchen where I knew Roland would be.

"Hello, my sweet boy," Roland said as he started to pet Koda. "You know he loves me better, right?" he teased as he looked right at me.

I couldn't help but roll my eyes.

"He only likes you because you slip him food from the table when you think

I'm not looking."

Roland was terrible at keeping Koda on his proper diet and schedule. He was always slipping him people food, even when he knew he wasn't supposed to be. It wasn't that Koda couldn't have a treat, but he had to earn it. He needed to work for it. That wasn't my rule, it was the rule for all of the working dogs.

"How was the trip?" Roland asked as he reluctantly moved away from Koda and opened his arms to give me a hug.

Roland was massive. It never failed to gain attention. He was twice my size and I wasn't a small guy. I had muscles and was more than capable of holding my own in a fight.

Roland had taught me how to fight. When I decided I wanted to be a federal agent, Roland had made sure I would be able to handle anything that came my way. He trained me in multiple fighting styles and shooting. He made sure I was ready for any fight.

We had a similar look, though, in terms of hair, eye color, and the shape of our face. You could tell by looking at us that we were brothers. We were both good looking and both gay. Though, unlike me, Roland took a long time to come out.

"Not bad. Airplanes are nothing for me. So what's been going on since we last spoke? You seem to be in a better mood than you were a few days ago. I expected to find you on the couch in sweatpants with empty pizza boxes and beer cans all around you."

When we had last talked, Roland was in a dark place. The guy that he liked, Tyler, hadn't spoken to him in a couple of weeks. He had also taken a week off of work.

It was the first time he had truly liked another guy since he had lost Shane. Shane was the man that he was madly in love with when he was younger and still in the Army.

Shane was out and proud, but Roland had been afraid to come out. Don't Ask, Don't Tell, was no longer in effect, but that didn't mean an organization flooded with alpha males would be open-minded about serving next to a gay man.

Roland had stayed in the closet and there was only so long Shane could handle it. One night, after an epic fight, Shane stormed off in the car, only to be hit by a drunk driver. Shane died on impact and the drunk driver got away. Roland then quit the Army and joined the

NYPD. He was the one that caught his lover's killer a few years later. Roland hadn't been in a relationship with anyone since.

"Tyler came over last night. We had a great conversation," he said, and flashed a warm smile.

"Oh, just a conversation?" I teased as I grabbed some coffee and headed for the table.

"A bit more than that. It started off with a conversation. He told me that he needed time to get his feelings in order and to process everything that had just happened."

"Makes sense, he thought he was straight his whole life. Having a guy kiss you out of nowhere can be shocking," I said with complete understanding to my voice.

"And that was my fault for doing it that way. It came out of nowhere. Thankfully, though, I didn't scare him off for very long. He told me he had feelings for me, too. That he didn't even sleep with the two women he had been dating in the past two months. He's actually never slept with a woman before, or anyone."

"Damn, you bagged yourself a twenty-two year old virgin. Now I'm jealous."

I was a sucker for a virgin or a spinner. I liked the smaller guys, the ones that you could toss around and overpower. I wasn't a fan of vanilla sex. I liked to have power over my lover. I liked to use toys and restraints. Sex was supposed to be fun and I believed in trying many different flavors of it. I tended to go for smaller guys, because they loved to bottom and I was only a top.

"The point is, we are taking things slow. We watched a movie and made out a bit last night before we went to sleep, in separate rooms. I'm trying to make him feel comfortable and allow him to stay in control of the sexual progress."

"I am happy for you. It's been a very long time since you've allowed yourself to be with another man. I know what happened with Shane was devastating, but you've kinda been putting your whole life on pause, Ro. I don't know what it's like to lose the man you love, and I didn't know him as well as I should have, but he wouldn't want this for you. He wouldn't want you to be alone and heartbroken for the rest of your life."

"I'm trying. What about you? Any new guy in your life?"

"Not right now, no. I've been too busy

with work. I'm not really the dating type, anyway. It's easier to keep things to friends with benefits or one-night stands."

I held zero interest in dating someone. With my job, it really wasn't even possible. I worked too many hours and I traveled all over the country at a moment's notice. It wasn't conducive to a healthy relationship.

"Always such a romantic," Roland teased, and once again I rolled my eyes.

Before I could comment, Koda's head snapped up and he looked right at the door. Instantly, I was on edge and ready for an attack. I knew it wasn't a normal reaction, but it was what always happened, now, when there was a knock at the door or the phone rang. I was always ready for an ambush and there was nothing I could do about it.

"You expecting someone?" I asked, doing my best to keep my voice calm and casual. I wasn't sure if I was able to pull it off.

"It's Isaiah, my friend with Social Services. He's coming by so we can talk about the foster home situation," Roland answered as he got up to let him in.

Roland had told me about Tyler, his current love interest, and his old partner, Jasper Monroe's reaction to each other. When he told me that Tyler seemed scared of his old foster father, I could tell it was bothering him.

Tyler had grown up in the foster care system and, for a couple of years, he'd had Monroe as his foster father. Monroe had never told Roland about it, not even after him and Tyler started to hang out. We both found their reactions to each other suspicious and decided that it should be looked into.

It wasn't common for a former foster child to have that much fear toward a foster father. Something had to have happened and I was worried what it was. I didn't want my brother to be caught in a deadly situation if it came back that Monroe was a dirty cop.

"Hey man, come on in," Roland said warmly as he opened the door.

I peeked around the corner so I could see what Isaiah looked like. I don't know what I was expecting for Isaiah, but I wasn't expecting what stood on the other side of the door. The man was a bit chubby and average looking, probably a teddy bear, but he looked like a wreck. Like he hadn't slept in days. I wasn't sure, but something was going on with him.

"Is your brother here?" he asked as he walked in.

"Yeah, in the kitchen. Come on back and grab a coffee. You look like you could use it."

"You wouldn't believe what I found, Roland," he said as they ambled toward the kitchen.

I had no idea what he had found, but by how he was behaving, he found something huge.

My gut said it was something I wasn't going to like.

"Mason, this is Isaiah. He works with Social Services and is who I reached out to about intel on Tyler," Roland said to me.

"It's nice to meet you," I said as I held my hand out for Isaiah to take.

He easily clasped my hand in his

before he spoke.

"Nice to meet you. I have a feeling we're going to need your help on this one."

I didn't like the sound of that. It was one thing to need a cop, but to need a federal agent, that meant something huge had happened.

"What did you find?" Roland asked, getting things started.

"I started by looking through Tyler's time with Jasper. As you know, he was there between the ages of twelve and fourteen. He was one of eight foster kids, sometimes a little less over the two years. On the surface, it all seems perfectly normal and there weren't any red flags in Tyler's file for Jasper. Before that, he had been through a lot of rough homes and had been abused. It all stopped for two years before he was sent to another foster home, and then it picked up all over again."

"Okay, but I'm not hearing anything to imply that something is wrong with Jasper. Sounds like you need to review all of the foster homes in the system, though," I said.

It wasn't uncommon for there to be a few bad apples within the foster home system. However, it sounded like they had more than a couple in this town.

"Tyler was diagnosed with a protein deficiency when he was eight. It makes it hard for him to gain weight. Aside from that, and the asthma, he was perfectly healthy. Broken bones and bruising, but no illnesses. For the two years he was with Jasper, everything was perfect. Too perfect. Bruises were gone, he went to school, everything was normal and without complaint. Then, all of a sudden, he is being transferred, by Jasper's request to another home and the hell started all over again. Only, he was there for two days when he started to get very sick. His social worker saw how sick he was and took him to the hospital. They ran his bloodwork and discovered he was going through cocaine withdrawal."

"Whoa, what?" Roland asked, shocked and outraged.

That wasn't good.

That confirmed that something more was going on within that foster home and it wasn't going to end well.

"There was no way of telling how it got into his system, just that it was there. His social worker asked where he got the drugs, but he clammed up. Jasper was brought in to be questioned, but he was a Detective, even back then, so the worker believed everything he said. He said Tyler must have gotten it from school, that he had no idea. They went with Jasper's story and never looked into his home or any of the other children."

"It's not uncommon for children in their young teenage years to get their hands on cocaine. I find it hard to believe that no one would have noticed. If he was going through physical withdrawals, he had to have been doing it for months and in large doses. Were any of the other children checked out?" I asked.

"That's the thing, the social worker never spoke to any of the current children or looked through his home. So, I did." He placed a rather large brown file on the table as he continued. "That is Jasper's and his wife, Dana's, fostering file. It includes every child they have ever taken in, including the current ones. Currently, he has nine kids all between the ages of nine and fourteen. I've started to go through the process of pulling the previous foster children's files, but there are over a hundred and fifty of them."

"Shit," Roland said, obviously shocked that it was that many.

That *was* a fast turnaround.

I knew that some homes kids came and went at one hell of a pace, however, that was usually in larger cities. The smaller cities, the kids tended to stay with their one foster parent unless something was wrong with them. Kids didn't tend to get passed around like Christmas candy in towns this size, as a general rule. There was no reason for Monroe to have that many previous children.

I was getting a bad feeling about this and it wasn't going to end well. Monroe was Roland's past partner. They were still partners when they needed backup on a case. This wasn't going to go well if Monroe was dirty, and it was starting to look like he was.

"It's going to take some time to pull all of their files and go through them to see if any doctor reports were made after their time with Jasper. Some were also moved to another city and I don't have access to their files," Isaiah continued.

"I can get 'em. I just need their names and I can pull the file, no matter where they were placed in the country. We need to do a sneak and peek at Monroe's house and see what is going on. I'm assuming you are operating under the impression that Monroe is cooking drugs in the house," I stated.

I had come here for a vacation, but I also knew that Roland was worried about Tyler. It was the least I could do after everything my brother had done for me.

"Last night, I looked through twenty files. Twelve of the kids were admitted to the hospital with withdrawal-like symptoms. Not all of them were given blood work. Most were told it was the flu and they would feel better in a few days. It's enough for me to make the hypothesis that cocaine is being either cooked at the house around the children, or the children were weighing and packaging the cocaine."

"That sounds like a reasonable hypothesis. I've never noticed any problems with Jasper being sick, though, in three years," Roland stated.

"Depends. I've gone into a lot of homes where the drugs were made in the basement and the kids were sick but the foster parents weren't. The kids were the ones touching the drugs and breathing it in as they were either cooking or packaging it. The parents were fine, because the ventilation system in the upstairs of the house was solid. It kept the fumes down in the basement and when they needed to go down there, they wore the proper protection. It's completely logical that Monroe isn't breathing it in. Just like it's logical that he is breathing it in, but he's never not been around it. His body could be addicted to it and he gets his fix by being in the house," I pointed out.

"Let's get the files and go through

them. See which kids were hospitalized after leaving Jasper's. I'll loop in Captain Perry so he's aware of the situation. Yes, we'll need to do a sneak and peek at his house. Mase, can you get a warrant from a judge? We gotta keep that out of town."

"I'll get it. With those files, we should have enough for a warrant," I said confidently. That was easy enough to do and I agreed that it needed to be out of town. A town this size, everyone knew everyone and no judge was going to give us a sneak and peek warrant with what we had.

"Okay, I have to go to the office and start pulling them. Do you want to join me there, or do you want me to bring them back here?" Isaiah asked.

"It would be better to do it here. We don't know who will talk to who. I want to try and keep this as quiet as possible," Roland answered.

"I'll be back in about an hour or so, then," Isaiah said, before he finished his coffee and headed out.

"I'll grab my bag and get my laptop out of it. I'll get A.S.A Crawford up to speed and he'll grab us a warrant," I said as I stood.

"Not exactly the vacation you were looking for. I'm sorry."

"It's okay. The drug cases are the easiest. Have you thought about just asking Tyler again? Tell him you know that Jasper could be mixed up with drugs."

It would make things easier if he talked to Tyler about it. It was most likely the reason why Tyler didn't want to talk about Monroe. That old fear was still inside of him, but if Roland could get him to open up, it would help a lot.

I might not be able to get a sneak and peek warrant with what we had. We might need Tyler to go on the record about what happened in that house to do something about it.

"No, I want to keep him out of this. I don't know what is going on, but I know that when drug dealers feel threatened, they'll attack the one they feel is responsible. I don't want Tyler getting hurt. It's better to leave him in the dark."

"It's your call. I'll support you in whatever you decide, Ro. I'll go grab my gear," I said with complete understanding to my voice.

I knew how dangerous drug dealers could be, especially with children. If he didn't want to bring Tyler into this just yet, that was his call and I would respect it.

Hopefully, we wouldn't need Tyler and I could secure us a warrant without anyone on record.

One thing was for certain, this wasn't the type of vacation I had been planning.

CHAPTER TWO

Jarod

I WAS BROUGHT out of my lovely dream by the annoying beeping sound coming from my alarm clock. Groaning, I rolled over and pulled the blanket over my head.

I wasn't a morning person. I wasn't even a mid-morning person. I was often up late at night reading something so I went to bed way too late for me to be able to be up at seven in the morning. I would normally hit the snooze until I was almost late, leaving myself only fifteen minutes to get ready and get out the door. The solution was moving my alarm clock to the other side of the room. That way, the only way to make the obnoxious beeping stop would be to get out of bed and physically turn it off. This morning, though, that was the last thing I wanted to do.

At twenty-five, you would think I would be happy and excited to start a new day. And maybe I would be if it weren't for the fact that my day consisted of being trapped in a tin can with a homophobic asshole that I would love to punch right in the mouth. I would never, though, because despite my desires and thoughts, I was still a timid person. I would never have the guts to punch my partner. Hell, I don't even have the guts to tell him to shut up. I don't exactly have the personality one would expect a cop to have, but I wasn't your typical cop, either. I was the smart guy in the room. I was the *smartest* guy in the room, actually. At least book wise speaking.

I didn't ask to be smart. It wasn't like I spent all of my free time studying growing up just to grow my IQ. I was a child prodigy. I didn't have a choice in if I was smart or not.

There were a lot of times where I was thankful for my IQ. Plenty of cases that I worked where it came in handy. I had a great solve rate and I even helped out with other police stations within the nearby towns. I never told anyone that, though, because I was not looking to make waves. My plan was to keep my head down and try to help as many people as I could without being noticed. It was a fine balance, but I was doing well with it.

There were more times than I would care to admit that I would have been happier to not be smart. I would have loved to be normal and be one of the guys. I would be able to fit in better. I would be able to understand some of their jokes that they all thought were hilarious. I would have loved to be able to just lie down and sleep without my mind going over everything.

It was why I was such a night owl. It was hard to get my mind to shut off at the end of the day. The only way I could make it shut off was by reading. Books had been my sanctuary throughout my life and I had no idea what I would do without them. I always had one with me. Sometimes it was a non-fictional book to help me learn more, and sometimes it was a fictional book. They weren't always in English, either. Some were in Spanish. I loved to read and I would read anything and everything.

I let out another groan as the beeping started to get faster. I vaguely wondered if it would explode one day. Forcing myself to finally get up, I pushed the blanket off my head and sat up. I picked up the book that I had been reading when I fell asleep and placed it on my bedside table. I then rubbed my hands over my face and climbed from the bed.

I smashed the off button on my alarm clock a bit too hard, but I was tired and I didn't care. Not this morning, anyway.

Seven in the morning was an ungodly hour and anyone that was a morning person had to be certifiable. That was the only logical explanation.

I hit the bathroom, did my business, brushed my teeth and washed my face. I quickly got dressed in the work clothes that'd I'd laid out the night before, making sure every thing looked neat and tidy. I made my way down to my kitchen and headed straight for my coffee maker.

I didn't have anything fancy in my life. I didn't care for high-end electronics or fancy clothes. There were only two things I cared about, my books and my coffee maker. It's why I had one that could be programmed to brew my coffee in the morning so it would be ready when I dragged my ass out of bed.

I grabbed my large to-go mug and

poured the coffee in before I added about six spoonfuls of sugar. I had been given crap about how I take my coffee for years, but I didn't care. I needed the sugar to help with the bitter taste. I'm not a fan of coffee because I like the taste. I'm a fan of coffee because it wakes me up. It was that simple.

I grabbed an apple from the basket on the table and then headed over to where I'd dropped my gun, badge, and keys on the sideboard when I came home last night. Strapping on the side holster and shoving my phone and badge into my front pants pocket, I was out the door and headed for work.

I didn't live too far from the station. Something I would like to correct once I had more money saved up. I wanted to purchase my own land so I had some space. I wanted peace and quiet, but also privacy.

I liked the idea of having space. I liked the thought of not being able to hear my neighbors. I would like to get a dog or two and enjoy their company. I could have a garden and grow my own fruit and vegetables. Have a couple of different apple trees. It would be peaceful and I couldn't wait until I could make that happen.

At the sight of the station, I felt my stomach drop. I hated being there. It sounded ridiculous because it was my job, but nonetheless, that's how it had become. I was a police detective. A good one, I thought.

It wasn't the job that I hated.

It was my partner.

Detective Baxter was a veteran

detective. He had been working as a cop for twenty-five years. He was an old timer with old-fashioned beliefs in and out of the department. He was a hard ass, and he didn't believe in people being able to change. He hated everyone that wasn't a white male, and he held zero patience for anyone who was the least bit different.

He was also one of the biggest homophobic assholes that I had ever met.

All day long, I got to hear about how much he hated gay people and why they all should be put into a camp or shot. It would be hard for anyone to listen to, yes, but when you were also one of those gay people that he hated, it wasn't easy to listen to and not react.

I wasn't exactly *out* at the station.

I always said I wasn't in the closet, but I wasn't partaking in any pride parades, either. I didn't believe in hiding who you were, but I also didn't believe in standing out. I didn't believe that anyone should have to tell people what their sexuality was and it shouldn't be the first thing that people see.

I wanted people to see that I was a capable detective. I didn't want anyone to assume that because I was gay that I was promoted to try and fill some type of quota. Not to mention I was half-spanish, so I already stood out among the ever-prominent white male crowd that made up the police force.

The only ally that I had in the station was Detective Roland Wright. He was openly gay and he had no idea that he had become my hero. He didn't hide that he was gay. He never allowed it to define him. He stood up for what he believed and he didn't care if someone didn't agree or like it.

The highlight, though, of my career so far, was when I got to witness Detective Wright knocking out Baxter in the break room just a couple weeks ago. It was the greatest moment of my life and a moment that I often replay in my head when I need a pick-me up.

That man was my hero.

I got out of my car and strolled inside with my coffee in hand. The station wasn't very busy. Most of the time the cops that worked here were out on the street either driving around or walking the street. We didn't get a lot of calls or emergencies here. It was mostly civil disputes that we would assist with. We had gangs in town, but unless you could catch them in the act, there wasn't much we could do.

It was hard for me, because I wanted to help. I wanted to be active and make the world a better and safer place, but all I could do was what was in my power to do in this town.

Most would argue that I could move to a bigger town, a place like New York, or even work for a federal agency. That wasn't possible for me. I couldn't go to a big town or become a fed.

Not with my past.

Or rather, my father's past I should say.

All I could do was what was in my power here in town. It would simply have to be good enough.

I made my way over to my desk that was off in the corner. I was the newest rookie detective and the privilege not only came with verbal degrading from everyone that outranked me, but also a tiny desk in the corner. Everyone's paperwork that they didn't want to do themselves always ended up on my desk. I knew I had to work through it and just wait until there was fresh meat for them to enjoy. Even once there was, I doubted I would stop being their punching bag.

I didn't fit in.

I was too smart and too shy and quiet.

They were all loud and not the brightest bulbs in the pack.

I slid into my chair and started to grab the first file that was placed on top of the pile and got to work. It was about ten minutes later when I was being interrupted by Baxter's voice, along with Jasper Monroe's.

I couldn't stand Jasper anymore than I could Baxter. There was just something off with Monroe. I didn't know what it was, but I'd never liked him. He'd always felt off to me. If one could feel evil and darkness, that is what Monroe felt like to me. I didn't like being around him, not when I could help it.

The problem was, Baxter and Monroe were best friends.

Not that they would call each other that, because according to them they were not thirteen year old girls.

"I'm telling you, Jas, you would not believe the set of tits on this woman," Baxter started, and it took everything in me not to roll my eyes.

"I can't believe you went to the strip club without me," Monroe complained.

"I thought your wife didn't like it when you went to the club."

"I can do whatever I want."

Idiots.

They were both sexist idiots and I didn't know how long I could sit there and listen to them. I flinched when I felt a ball of paper hit the side of my head. I looked up to see both of them smirking at me.

"What about you, Rookie? What's the biggest pair of tits that you've seen?" Monroe asked with a smirk.

Too many times I'd had to deal with them asking me about my sexual conquests. It didn't matter how many times I'd told them it wasn't any of their business, they kept asking me.

"I don't kiss and tell." I had lost count how many times I'd told them the exact same sentence.

"I'm starting to think you've never been kissed so you have nothing to tell, Rookie," Monroe teased.

"Or maybe he has kissed, but he's been kissing fags like Wright," Baxter said with a disgusted look on his face.

"Naw, he don't look like a fudge eater. We should take him to the club, let him get a ride on a stripper. Get his willy wet and maybe he won't be so damn boring," Monroe said before he gave a chuckle.

The last thing I would be doing was going to a strip club with them. Thankfully, I was saved from further conversation when Monroe got a call on his cell phone.

I couldn't help but notice that he had a different cell phone. He normally had a black shiny one, but this one was black with a matte finish. It was also a tiny bit bigger. He obviously got a new cell phone within the past couple of days. I shrugged it off as just one more thing that was none of my business.

Monroe didn't answer the call right there, though. He got up and walked off before he even hit the button. That was strange, but it could have been his wife.

I pushed it off to the back of my mind and turned my attention back to the stack of paperwork. If I wanted to get out of here today, I needed to make a serious dent in the pile.

CHAPTER THREE

Mason

"ALL RIGHT, I got the no knock warrant," I said as I walked into the tactical room at the station.

I had been there for two weeks since I had arrived in town for my time off. Two weeks of me helping Roland and Isaiah try and figure out what was going on with the foster system. This wasn't what I was supposed to be doing and yet, I was here helping. At the end of the day, Roland needed help and I needed the distraction.

I had been staying with Roland for the past two weeks and, so far, he hadn't noticed that anything was different about me. It helped that he almost never slept, so for me to be up with him, it didn't raise any red flags. I had been trying to get a sneak and peek warrant, but we didn't have enough intel. No matter what circumstantial evidence we had, it wasn't good enough. Not when we were looking to get a judge to approve of a sneak and peek warrant for a decorated police detective.

All of that changed when Roland had spoken with his boyfriend, Tyler, last night and got him to tell his story on the record. I couldn't believe what I heard when he played it this morning at the station for me and his Captain.

Captain Perry.

Monroe not only had his foster children cooking the cocaine, he had also killed the ones that became too sick or were looking to talk. On top of that, he had sold other children into the sex trade when it suited his needs or when he needed to get rid of a child.

This sick fuck was making hundreds of thousands off of these children and it needed to end.

Thankfully, that recording was all I needed to get a judge to sign off on the warrant. Tonight, we were going to be raiding Monroe's home that he shared with his wife, Dana.

We had to be careful with the children being in the home, though. The last thing we needed was Monroe feeling threatened and hurting one of the children.

We called every detective in the police force to come in to help with the arrests. We also had Isaiah sticking around so he could handle the children. The problem was, the other cops in the police force had no idea that anyone had been looking into Monroe.

He was a decorated and well loved detective. He had been there for a very long time and he was highly respected. We were about to reveal to them that he was a monster and he needed to be taken out. It wasn't going to go over well and it would be a shock.

I just hoped it wouldn't blow back on Roland.

"We brief everyone in ten," Captain Perry said in a tense voice, before he headed out of the room.

I couldn't blame the man. This was his station and he'd had a dirty cop working underneath him since day one and he never suspected anything. I couldn't hold it against him. This was a small town, things like this weren't supposed to happen.

I knew it could, though. I had seen it plenty of times while being on the job. It wasn't always major towns that had the worst monsters. Sometimes, the smaller the town the worse the monsters were. They took comfort in the fact that the town was so small. They could fool everyone and be free to hurt anyone they wanted because no one ever looked at one of their own as a monster when something went wrong.

I started to grab the tactical gear I

would need, as I hadn't brought any with me.

"What about Koda?" Isaiah asked. He seemed uncomfortable being around this many guns. He was a man that cared about peace more than the violence that it takes to bring peace.

"I'll bring him with me so he can help with the children. We have no idea what the kids are going to be like. Do you have transport for the children?" I responded as I started to get ready.

"I have a fellow social worker on standby with a van to transport the children to the hospital. I haven't found new placements yet, though. I wanted to see what their condition was and if they have any cocaine in their system first. Chances are they will, and they'll need to stay in the hospital for at least a week.

What about the other children, though? The ones that were sold. We can't just forget about them."

That was going to be harder. Selling a child wasn't like buying a piece of fruit from the store. They didn't get a receipt for their purchase and the seller didn't have to claim it on their taxes. Children were traded for cash, diamonds, drugs... hell, even bitcoin, now. It made it extremely difficult to track and even if we did find who the original buyer was, that kid could have been sold twelve additional times before we even found the first one. It was a nightmare, and that was before we factored in that a child could be out of the country.

"I've already contacted my boss about the situation down here. He's going to talk to the Governor about what can be done,"

I answered.

I wasn't sure what was going to happen. Chances were everything would be passed off to a federal agency to try and work the case. At the end of the day, it would be one more case file to the ever-growing pile. Unless those kids were found in a raid, we were never going to find them.

"Let's go get this bastard," I said as I snapped the clip into my gun.

We all moved out and walked into the small briefing room that also worked as the roll call room. It was a small police station, but I had been in smaller.

It was a perk to be a federal agent that traveled all over the country. I could find a spot to work anywhere, no matter how big or small the police station was.

Captain Perry was already in the room,

ready and waiting for us. We moved over to the side of the room to give Captain Perry our full attention.

"Before we begin, I want to make one thing very clear, this is not a training exercise. You are the more experienced detectives that I have. Some of you have never done a raid before outside of a training exercise. The majority of you have only ever done one or two raids when a nearby town needs more bodies. Due to the type of raid that we are about to go on, I am going to rely on experience to lead us. Detective Wright and his brother, Special Agent Mason Wright, they will be taking point on this raid. I expect everyone to follow their orders and do as they tell you, myself included. What matters most is that we all come home alive and no one gets killed tonight. Do I make myself clear?"

Several heads nodded amid a shuffling of feet. Everyone in the room had a serious look on their face, but I could tell that some didn't think much of this. They were expecting this to be a simple little raid.

They had no idea what was coming their way.

"Keep an eye on Baxter, tonight. I don't know if he'll be a team player," Roland whispered to me.

Roland had told me about Baxter. He had punched him a while back when Baxter wouldn't shut up about gay police officers. Roland had become sick and tired of hearing Baxter's homophobic bullshit and finally knocked his ass out.

I didn't really need Roland to tell me *why* he felt I needed to keep an eye on the man. If Baxter was that old fashioned that he didn't believe in gay cops or even female cops, then he might not want to believe a fellow detective was doing this to children.

The old timers were always the hardest to convince, because they were brought up on the blue wall. You never betray or rat out a fellow brother in blue, no matter what it was. We were about to arrest one. It could get ugly if the old timers wanted to make it that way.

"We have secured a no knock warrant for the home of one of our own, Jasper Monroe. He has been under investigation for the past few weeks for suspected drug trafficking. We secured the warrant based on an eyewitness account of drugs being produced in his house in the basement. We also have evidence of him killing foster children or selling them to pedophiles for close to two decades. We have an arrest warrant for Jasper and his wife, Dana," Captain Perry continued.

"You expect us to believe that one of our own, a cop who has almost thirty years on the job, is not only a drug dealer, but a child killer? Who is this eyewitness, Santa Claus?" Baxter asked, clearly not believing anything Captain Perry had to say.

I expected as much from Baxter. But what was interesting was the kid next to him, the unsurprised look on his face. I knew Jarod was Baxter's partner. I had seen him around the station over the past two weeks, but we had never spoken. Hell, I'd never heard him speak to anyone. He seemed to always be on his own.

"Why doesn't the kid seem surprised?"

I whispered to Roland.

"He's only been a detective for a year, but he joined the police force at eighteen. He's only twenty-five and has a shit load of potential. I don't know anything else about him other than he keeps everything personal under wraps. He's smart, though. Smarter than he wants people to know. He could have easily seen something," Roland whispered back.

That was interesting. I love smart people. They had a way of seeing the world that everyone else couldn't. Smart people, they could see through the world and that was a huge asset to have in an investigation.

"The witness' identity is being kept a secret for obvious reasons. We have more than enough evidence to back up the claims. Once we get into the house, we'll find the lab in his basement. He currently has nine foster children that we will need to ensure are safe before they are transported to the hospital for evaluations. Due to the nature of this investigation, all cell phones will be left here in the station. I don't want anyone reaching out to either Jasper or Dana. Agent Wright, you wished to say something," Captain Perry said with a pointed look at me.

I didn't have anything to say.

I didn't *want* to say anything, but apparently Captain Perry felt otherwise. I moved to the front of the room and gave the typical speech.

"Due to the connection Jasper has to this police department, his charges will be placed by Homeland Security, making them federal charges. He will be eligible for the death penalty, which means anyone that tries to contact him or help him in any way will be charged with aiding and abetting a wanted criminal, as well as an accessory after the fact. You will be facing hard time in a federal prison and I will personally ensure you are placed in gen pop and not solitary." I paused to allow the seriousness of the situation to sink in before I continued.

"We are going to hit his home in two teams. Roland's team will hit the front door and my team will hit the back and hold down the perimeter. Once the arrests have been made, Isaiah will then handle the children. If you cannot do your job, then speak up now, because once we leave, you will have no choice but to do your job and ensure that Jasper does not evade arrest."

"You heard him, does anyone want to be kept here?" Captain Perry asked.

I was waiting to see someone raise their hand, but surprisingly no one did. They weren't happy, but they were riding with us. I knew there would be hard feelings, though, and this would be talked about once they were allowed. It was going to be the talk of this whole fucking town for months to come.

With nothing else to say, we all started to get ready. Phones were placed in a basket before we made our way to the cars and headed off.

I rode in the vehicle with Roland and a few other detectives. The atmosphere in the car was tense, to say the least. No one talked, not that I expected anyone to. They all just had a bomb dropped on them so, right then, something like small talk wasn't important. That was perfectly fine with me. I wasn't in the mood to talk any more than they were.

This was a lot for me to be taking in. I was wearing tactical gear that was not mine. I was using a gun that was not mine. I hated this and the slight feel of anxiety started to creep up my spine.

I was supposed to be getting a break from all of this. I had taken a month off from work to escape and relax. To take the time and get my head on straight. I wasn't down here to work a case. To go on a raid with a bunch of cops that would have loved for me to not be here. This was the farthest thing from stress free and relaxing that you could get.

Pulling up to the house, we all got out of our vehicles and instantly made our way into position with our respective teams. While Roland ran with his team to the front of the house, I went to the back of the house. In my team, I had Jarod and his asshole partner, Baxter, with me.

Yup.

I was just that lucky.

I looked at my team and I could see that most of them looked about ready to throw up. They were not prepared for this mentally, whatsoever. They most likely had only done this in a training exercise and I knew that was far from the real thing, especially if bullets started to fly. Real bullets that could kill you and not the dummy rounds that just burned.

"Remember, there are kids in the house and in the basement there will be chemicals that can explode if hit with a bullet. When we breach, I will stay out here with Lopez in case anyone runs out the back. The rest of you go in and start clearing the house. Based on the blueprints, the access to the basement is closer to us, so go down first and secure the children."

They all gave a nod in unison and then I heard the Captain's voice over the coms giving the all clear to breach. The others went in and I stood at the ready, facing the backdoor with Jarod to my right.

I knew it would have made more sense for me to be going in, but I wasn't certain the person I left out here wouldn't let Monroe leave. I had to make sure if he ran out the back, that we would get him.

I could feel the tension radiating off of Jarod. I had no idea why he was so tense and nervous. He should feel the safest, really. He was outside and he had me with him. Even if he doubted his own skills, I was a federal agent and that generally made local police feel better in the field.

"You all right?" I asked, without taking my eyes off of the door.

"I'm fine, Sir," Jarod said in a tight voice.

"No offense, but you aren't radiating fine." I should have let it go. It wasn't any of my business what his problem was. He said he was fine, and I should drop it. For some reason, though, I didn't want to.

"I have no problem arresting Monroe, Sir. I'm upset about the children. They shouldn't have to go through this. Children are supposed to believe in superheroes and magic. They are supposed to believe monsters are mythical creatures that don't exist. They aren't supposed to know the truth yet,

Sir."

I couldn't agree more. Children were supposed to be innocent, but millions all over the world were living in hell and no one was coming to save them. I had been working hard to try and save as many as I could, but always felt like the more I saved, the more who got thrown into hell. It was an endless war and it would never end.

It was why so many agents on my unit burned out so quickly. It was a tough life to live. It was hard to see the worst that humanity had to offer, but stepping away from that, to me, it felt like I was turning my back on all of those children and that wasn't something I could live with.

"You can drop the *Sir*. And you're right. They aren't supposed to know about this yet, but they do, and it's our job as adults to save them and try to get them help. That's all we can do."

It was a moment later when the children started to file out of the house, guided by some of the officers on my team. They all looked sick and I knew they were in for a long recovery after all of this.

"Monroe isn't here," a detective informed me as he moved on with the children.

"Fuck." I grabbed the radio. "House is cleared, Monroe isn't here."

Monroe was on the run, most likely.

It was late at night.

He should have been here.

I couldn't help but wonder if someone had said something. If someone had gotten wind of what we were trying to do, tipped him off, and Monroe took a runner.

I made my way to the front of the house and went over to where Captain Perry was standing. I saw Roland making his way over as well, after putting Dana into the squad car.

"She give anything up?" I asked, once he was close enough.

"Apparently, he's away on a surprise boys weekend," Roland answered.

"Bullshit," I instantly said.

"He's up to something. You think he caught wind of the investigation?" Captain Perry asked.

"Someone who has almost thirty years of experience on the job holds a lot of connections. There's no telling who he could have heard something from. Could have been someone within Social Services. It would make sense that he had a mole on the inside. Someone that could feed him the children that no one would think twice about going missing. Someone to help cover it all up. He could have been made aware of the investigation once files started getting pulled," I stated.

"Shit. And now he's in the wind," Roland said as he shook his head.

"Detective Wright, Sir," Jarod said with an uncertain voice as he made his way over to us. He was clearly nervous about walking in on our conversation, but he seemed determined to do it. He was holding a folded up piece of paper in his hand and he spoke as he held it out to me.

"One of the children said he was told to give this to you."

"What is it?" Captain Perry asked as Roland grabbed the paper.

The second he opened the note, I could

see all of the color drain from his face. Something was on that piece of paper that none of us were going to like.

"Roland, what is it?" I asked, now on edge.

"Tyler," he said, before he took off for his car.

I grabbed the note and gave it a quick read. I knew exactly what made Roland's blood run ice cold. I passed the note off to Captain Perry as Koda and I took off to join Roland in his car before he had a chance to run off.

There was no way I was going to allow my brother to potentially go into a trap. I was going to have his back, no matter what. The note itself was simple, but the words were already circling around my head, haunting me as every second passed that we spent in the car.

It's your fault for him breaking the rules. Dead men tell no tales, Wright.

CHAPTER FOUR

Mason

WE ARRIVED AT the bar that Tyler worked at to find it engulfed in flames.

I could feel the fear radiating off of Roland and I hated that I couldn't make it better.

The second we were out of the car, though, my fear escalated when Koda instantly started to run toward the building. He was trained to help, to save, and when he saw the fire and smelled a person inside, he ran like he was trained to do. It was why he, normally, had to be kept on a leash that was attached to my hip unless I released him. I hadn't done that, though, because he typically stayed with me unless ordered to do otherwise, even in a firefight. Both Roland and I ran after Koda and into the bar.

The whole place was covered in flames and smoke. A bar was the worst place to have a fire because of all the alcohol. It only fueled the flames and made them eat everything in their path. We could barely see anything and the smoke was so thick it was hard to breathe.

"Koda!" I yelled out to try and find him.

A set of sharp barks hit our ears and I instantly ran in his direction. I found him on the other side of the bar, along with Tyler. Tyler had one of the shelves that fell from the back of the bar trapping him on the floor and, not wasting any time or thought to my own safety, I was quickly removing it, just as Roland arrived.

"Get him up," I said as I moved the heavy shelf.

Koda had latched on to Tyler's wrist and he and Roland pulled Tyler from under the shelf as I lifted. Once he was free, I dropped the shelf as Roland scooped up Tyler into his arms. I snatched Koda up in my arms and carried him as we all ran out.

I could feel the heat from the fire on the bottom of my feet and I was wearing boots. The floor was way too hot for Koda's paws to handle for long. The second we made it outside we all started to cough and Koda whined in my arms.

An ambulance was already here and I watched as Roland placed Tyler down on the stretcher. Something was wrong, though, because Tyler kept coughing and he wasn't able to open his eyes. I stood back and watched as the paramedic had to intubate him.

I could see the fear and worry in Roland's eyes and I hated that I couldn't make it better for him. The man that he was in love with was struggling to breathe. There was nothing I could say that would make it better for him.

He looked back at me as they loaded the stretcher into the ambulance. I gave him a nod to assure him it was okay and that I would be fine. That was all he needed before he climbed into the ambulance and it drove away.

"It'll be okay, boy," I said to Koda as I carried him over to the squad car. The dog gave a weak whine once more that tugged at my heart. I needed to look at his paws and make sure he didn't have any burns that I needed to tend to.

Just as I placed him down in the back seat of the car, my phone beeped with a text message. I pulled it out and saw that it was my boss. He was in town and wanted to meet. It seemed like my night was just getting better and better.

CHAPTER FIVE

Jarod

THIS WAS UNREAL.

I knew it was true, but it was all so unreal to me. I had no idea when I was called into help with a raid that it would be an actual raid. I had done a few training drills and it was all the same. They came in at random times and days to help make it more authentic. To help you be ready for when that call could come in. I enjoyed doing the training exercises, though. It always made me feel like I was being a real cop. Only, this wasn't a drill, it was an actual raid for not only a criminal, but one of our own.

I had always suspected that Monroe was dirty. I never had any proof and even if I did, I doubted that anyone would listen or believe me.

The raid wasn't what I thought it would be. I don't really know what I expected, exactly, but that wasn't it. It annoyed me that I was kept outside instead of going in.

If anyone shouldn't have gone in, it should have been Baxter.

There was no way he would believe that Monroe had done anything wrong. I knew that even seeing the children and the drug lab, Baxter would have blown it off as a coincidence. Tried to make it seem like it was all Dana and Monroe was completely innocent in it all. As if a detective with close to thirty years of experience would miss the cocaine lab in his basement.

I shouldn't have been kept outside. I felt like they were babying me, putting the rookie in the corner so he couldn't be hurt. I was a good detective and I was trained just like the rest of them. I took extra courses in tactical advantages, hand-to-hand, and shooting. I made sure I would be ready, no matter what came my way. It wasn't just that, I loved to learn and I didn't really care what I learned as long as I could put it into play to help others.

Finally allowed to go in the house, I

pulled out a pair of black latex gloves and made my way back to the door and slipped inside. Dana had been taken to the station and the Wright brothers headed out of here in a panic once I handed them that note. I had read it and I knew they would be going to find Tyler.

I had overheard Detective Wright talking about him quietly to his brother. Everyone seemed to always forget I was around, that I could hear. It was a fact that I had been using to my advantage to collect intel from everyone I worked with. Monroe was on the run and I was willing to bet there had to be a clue in this house somewhere that could lead us to where he was.

"Find anything?" I asked Baxter as I made my way into the basement after putting on a mask.

MASON

Even with the mask, I could smell the fumes from the chemicals down there. I couldn't believe the children had been down there working without a mask. It was too intense for me and I was a grown ass adult. There was no telling what would be wrong with the children.

"Just chemicals. It doesn't mean anything," Baxter said, and I could tell he was in denial.

"They're not making breath mints down here," I commented before I could stop the words from coming out of my mouth. It was the wrong thing to say, I knew that, but it just slipped out.

Baxter instantly turned around, and before I could even register what was happening, a hard right cross hit my jaw and I stumbled into the wall.

That was going to bruise.

It wasn't the first time I had taken a hit, but it was the first time my partner had hit me. At least, someone that was supposed to be my partner.

"Jasper is a good man. He isn't involved in this and there is nothing in this place or what someone could say that would make me believe it," he said with an edge to his voice before he stormed off.

Yeah, he's a real good man.

That was why he had nine children around dangerous chemicals.

Why there's testimony from a witness that saw him kill and sell children.

It was all a coincidence or some type of ploy to take down a good man.

I rolled my eyes and let out a sigh.

It was bullshit and, eventually, Baxter was going to have to wake up and face the facts. The trick was, if Monroe knew

Baxter would be willing to help him flee, Baxter might be going down as well by the end of this investigation. Letting out another sigh, I turned my full attention to the room. There had to be something in this house that could help and I was determined to find it.

CHAPTER SIX

Jarod

IT HAD BEEN less than twenty-four hours since we had done the raid on Monroe's house.

I had stayed there for a good six hours combing through everything, but there wasn't anything that would indicate where Monroe would have run to.

Everything I found only linked back to

Dana.

I suspected that was Monroe's whole plan. He wanted to make sure his wife was left holding the bag. It only further proved what type of man he was. He wasn't even brave enough to face the consequences of his own actions. Instead, he made sure it all connected back to his wife so she would have to take the full ride. With all of the evidence connecting back to her, it would be harder for the prosecutor to pin the crimes on Monroe.

Any defense attorney could argue that Dana was the culprit and ringleader. That Monroe had no idea anything sinister was happening within the house. It wouldn't get him off entirely, but it could drastically reduce his charges and he could actually end up on probation instead of spending the rest of his life in jail.

It was a mess.

That was the only way to describe it.

I made my way through the hospital to go up to the pediatric floor so I could check in on the children. I was hoping they might be able to tell me something that we could use to not only find Monroe, but charge him with everything. These children were witnesses and they needed to be protected until we got Monroe in custody.

I made my way to the playroom where some of the children were set to be. I had reached out to Isaiah, their social worker, to let him know I was looking to speak with some of the children. I knew Isaiah had to be there during the questioning with them not having any parents.

I walked into the playroom and saw

that there were only two children there. They didn't look too healthy, either. I knew they were from Monroe's house because we were using one of the playrooms strictly for the children that we saved last night.

The hospital had been good about closing this room off to the other children so we could do interviews in a more friendly environment. These two looked to be the older children out of the nine that we saved. I knew who they were. I made a point of knowing everything that I could about the children we rescued. I didn't want them to feel like I didn't care enough about them to even learn their names. I had no idea what they were feeling, though. I had never gone through the foster system. I was lucky in that sense.

My parents weren't amazing. Hell, I

grew up being ignored and treated as an inconvenience, but I didn't have to grow up not knowing who I would be living with or where I would be sleeping at night. I didn't have to go through the horrors that so many children experience within the foster system. I didn't have a picture perfect childhood, not even close to it, but I didn't have to be afraid all day and night long. I had never been touched sexually or abused physically. I wasn't wanted or loved, but I came out of my childhood without any major scars.

Isaiah came over to me and I held my hand out for him as I spoke.

"Afternoon."

"Hey, any news yet?" Isaiah asked as he shook my hand.

"Not yet, no. I'm hoping to get something out of these guys."

"You can try, but others have already asked. No one is giving anything up. They all keep saying it was Dana."

"Okay," I said, giving him a nod before I made my way over to the kids.

I sat down on the rug with them. I wanted them to feel like I was on their side and not on a different level than them. I didn't want to intimidate or scare them, either.

"Hey guys, my name is Detective Lopez, but you can call me Jarod. I was hoping I could talk to you both about what has been going on," I started calmly.

"Dana had us working on the drugs. Mr. Monroe is a good man and he didn't know about anything going on in the house," Jeff said in a dead tone. He was twelve and one of the oldest out of the nine kids.

"Isaiah has told me that everyone seems to be saying that. But let me ask you guys this, how is it possible that Mr. Monroe didn't know about the drugs or about the abuse?" I asked next.

"He works a lot and when he is home we keep to ourselves and stay away from him so he doesn't know about it," Chris answered this time. He was thirteen, and the oldest amongst the nine kids. I suspected he was the group's protector, given that he had more injuries than the others. Both Chris and Jeff weren't going through withdrawals yet, so they had a lot of cocaine in their system built up. It also meant once the withdrawals started to hit, it would be hard on the both of them.

"But he's a detective, why didn't anyone tell him about what was going on?" I asked next.

"Dana made sure we never talked. It was safer for the other kids if we stayed quiet," Jeff answered.

"I don't know what you want us to say, but Mr. Monroe had nothing to do with anything that went on in the house. He didn't know. He's a good man and would never do anything to harm a child. You won't get us to say otherwise," Chris said with conviction to his voice.

They did everything they could to protect the younger children and they still were. I had a feeling they were scared that Monroe would do something to them. They were most likely threatened with death if they ever talked and Monroe found out about it. Even after he was out of the picture, they were still too scared to cross that line and say anything against him. None of the kids would and pressing them to tell us the truth would only make them worse.

"Okay, I appreciate you guys speaking with me. Do you think it's okay if I hang out for a little bit with you guys?"

I didn't want to just leave and make them feel like they weren't important. I wanted them to know that we were on their side, even if they couldn't tell us the truth. And maybe, spending time with them would help to build up some trust and they just might talk or let something slip. They both gave a nod before they went back to building with the smaller Lego pieces.

I looked over at Isaiah and gave him a nod to let him know I wouldn't be questioning them anymore. He gave a nod and headed out.

I spent the next fifteen minutes

hanging out with Jeff and Chris. I was casually building something with the Lego to try and build some type of a connection with the boys when the door opened.

The sound of the door opening had caused them both to flinch and I knew it was ingrained into them.

"It's okay, he's a cop," I assured them when I saw Agent Wright.

He was technically a federal agent, but I didn't want to scare them anymore than they already were. I also noticed that Agent Wright's dog was here with him as well. His dog had some gauze wrapped around his paws, presumably from the fire last night. I had heard about what happened to Tyler at the bar. Everyone in the station was talking about it.

We all suspected that Tyler was the eyewitness to Monroe's crimes and he was looking to take him out. Tyler was the one adult that could put Monroe in an active role of what happened at the house. It only made sense for Monroe to want to eliminate Tyler and better his odds. It didn't work, though, as the Wright brothers were able to get to the bar and save Tyler before it was too late.

"Hey guys, how are you feeling?" Agent Wright asked, as his dog walked over to us and, to my surprise, lay down next to me.

I loved dogs, but I knew that working dogs always stayed by their partner. I didn't expect for the dog to come to me and just lay down right next to me. I reached over and gave him pets as Chris spoke on behalf of him and Jeff.

"We're fine."

"We were just seeing what we could

build out of these Legos," I said, but I shook my head slightly so Wright would know that they didn't want to talk.

I was hoping he would understand and not press them for answers they were never going to give. He gave me a small nod in return and I knew he understood me.

"I just wanted to check in on you guys. Koda was also really worried about you."

"That your dog?" Jeff asked.

"He is. He's my partner. He goes everywhere with me to help me protect children, like yourselves. He rescued someone from a fire last night, so his paws are a bit sore."

"Will he be okay?" Chris asked, with a hint of worry for Koda's welfare lacing his voice.

"He'll be okay in a couple of days. We'll

leave you to your building. Come, Koda."

Koda tilted his head up and looked over at Agent Wright for a brief moment before he placed his head back down on his paws. He held zero interest in moving and I could tell, based on the slight look of shock that went through Agent Wright's eyes, this was a first for him. He was used to Koda always listening to his commands. For some reason, though, Koda didn't want to leave.

I suspected it had to do with the children.

Dogs were very attuned to children and their emotions. He would be able to pick up on them being hurt and scared.

"Looks like he wants to hang out with us. We can keep an eye on him, right boys?" I asked them, flashing a warm smile.

"I'm very good with animals. I don't mind watching him," Jeff easily agreed.

"All right, if you're sure. I'll come by shortly to pick him up," Agent Wright said.

I could tell he felt uneasy about it. He liked having Koda by his side and I suspected he felt like a piece of him was missing when he wasn't. K9s and their partners were supposed to share a very strong and special bond. A bond that was deep and unwavering. It made sense that he would prefer to have Koda around him.

If I hadn't known it before, I knew then that Agent Wright was a good man and I had more respect for him than ever. He was going to push himself through the discomfort just so he could help provide some comfort to the boys. I gave him a warm smile, hoping that would help ease some of his discomfort, and he returned the smile before he strolled out.

With Koda here, I hoped that maybe the boys would open up more and I could get something out of them that I could use to find Monroe. I was determined to find him and I would not rest until I did.

CHAPTER SEVEN

Mason

THIS WAS A shit show.

That was the only way I could think to describe the situation. I was supposed to be coming down here on vacation. This was supposed to be my time off. My time to get my head back on straight and try to fix myself. This was not the time for me to be going after an evil man that enjoyed using children to cook drugs and killing the ones that became too troublesome. This wasn't what I was supposed to be doing. I was trying to get a break. A break I desperately needed and, now, I was roped into this. I'd committed myself despite the fact that I really did know better. It was too late to turn around and ignore it all. I *had* to help, it was who I was, what I did. That didn't change that I wasn't mentally prepared for it.

I pulled up to the rest stop just thirty minutes outside of town. My boss, Special Agent in Charge, Derek Keyes, wanted to talk with me. I knew he wasn't happy about losing Jasper Monroe. Monroe was a serious offender and he was also a cop, or, well, ex-cop, now. That made him a huge offender that needed to be brought to justice. Now that everyone at the station knew that Monroe was a dirty cop and on the run, Roland was safe in the sense that his fellow cops knew the truth. But he and Tyler wouldn't truly be safe until Monroe was in custody or dead.

Koda whined and I reached over to give him a quick pat on the head before I got out of my truck and made my way over to Keyes, who perched on top of a picnic table at the edge of the rest stop, a good way from the doors to the small coffee shop there. It was getting dark out, but it was quiet and we were alone. I went and hopped up next to him as I spoke.

"Boss."

"How are you doing, Wright?"

"We lost Monroe. We recovered the children, but there are more buried somewhere that we'll need to find. His wife is going to jail, though. The piece of shit did a runner and left her holding the bag."

"He needs to be found. But there is also a problem with the foster care system in that town. It's not normally our jurisdiction, however, the Governor has decided to make it our jurisdiction. His order is that I assemble a task force that will operate in Gaithersburg to ensure the foster system in that town is corrected."

"Their own police and social workers can do that. Why would the Governor want a special task force?"

It seemed ridiculous to have a task force organized just to handle something that could be done through town. They didn't need federal agents, especially for something like that.

"The task force will be made up of federal agents and local police, but also social workers. The primary objective is to help to correct the foster care system in town, but the team will be going after the most violent offenders for crimes against children. The local boys don't have enough experience on their own to handle this. They need someone experienced in the field to lead the team. The social workers will help to place the children recovered from the takedowns in secure foster homes or back with their family. It's going to be a major undertaking, but will lead to saving a great deal of children. The task force is being given special privileges by the Governor. The Governor cares about results and not necessarily the means to get there. He is offering complete immunity to everyone working in the new task force. Now, that is, within reason. Obviously, if one of the members commits murder, sexual assault, or a crime against a minor there wouldn't be any immunity and they'd be prosecuted. Everything else will be at the discretion of the task force leader."

I wasn't expecting that. I knew the Governor was looking to lower the crime rates against children. Almost every politician gives the same speech about reducing crime rates, but very few of them try to do something about it. Apparently, the Governor was sick of waiting around for others to jump on the cause. If the task force was successful enough, he could easily rise in the political race. It was a smart call for him to make career wise. It might sound cold, but if it meant that more children would be saved from horrific crimes, that was all that mattered.

"A lot of responsibility for one person. Is that why you're here? You moving?"

"Hell no. I like New York. The Governor has allowed me to choose who will run the task force. I'm choosing you."

"What?"

How many ways could I say *hell no*?

I speak three languages in addition to English, so I could really say it a lot of different ways. I was not going to be running any task force. I didn't care what he had to say.

That was way too much responsibility.

I wasn't ready for it.

There were plenty of guys older than me, more experienced than me, who could run it. I was only seven years in. I wasn't ready to run something of this magnitude. I wouldn't even know where to start.

"You are the perfect agent to run this

task force, Wright. I am promoting you to Supervisory Special Agent. You will select your team from any active federal agent. You will also get to decide on who joins you from the local police and the social workers that you want to bring into the task force. Your first objective is to find Jasper Monroe and bring him to justice."

"You are making it sound like I don't have a choice."

"Because you don't. It's a direct order. This task force is yours to run. If you succeed, you save a lot of innocent children. If you fail, your career will be over and you will have failed a lot of innocent children," he said, his tone firm and brooking no argument. He sat back with a shrug.

The fact that he could dictate the order as easily as if we were talking about the weather told me how serious this was. Keyes always got like this when everything was on the line. He tried to downplay it by talking nonchalantly about it. As if that would somehow ease the gut punch he sent your way.

I didn't like this.

I didn't like that I wasn't getting a say in my own career.

I didn't like that I was being thrown into the deep end with this task force. I had no idea what I was going to do or how to run a task force. And now, I was going to have to figure it out whether I wanted to or not, regardless if I felt out of my depth.

"How do I select the people for the task force?"

"You have access to the federal agent database, look them over and see who pops out for you. I would recommend choosing people who have a great reputation, and that you think bring something to the task force. You will want to focus on different areas. At minimum, you're going to want a tech specialist, a sniper, someone who is well rounded all across the board, a hand-to-hand specialist, a smart guy. You know, figure out who would help make the task force better. Focus on people that bring something unique to the table that will help you catch more criminals. It's a specialized unit that you are building, Wright. You got this."

At least he was confident, because I wasn't. This was too much responsibility for me to be taking on, especially right now. I was supposed to be on leave. I was supposed to be able to have a break and now, I was being thrown back into action when I wasn't certain I was ready. I couldn't tell Keyes that, though, because then I could kiss my career goodbye. I had to endure and hope I didn't screw this up.

"Any other bombs you'd like to drop on me?"

"No, that was it. I gotta head back. You got this, Wright," Keyes said again as he slid off the picnic table and casually strolled away toward his car.

I didn't have this.

There was no way in hell I was going to be able to pull this off.

Could I find Monroe, sure, that was simple, that wasn't anything I hadn't done a hundred times before.

But could I run a team?

Could I chase down leads and do whatever it took to bring down different criminal organizations as the lead agent?

I doubted it. I was only seven years in. Sure, there had been a lot that I had learned, but there were still a great number of things that I didn't know.

Things that only experience and time could teach.

In the field, you rely on someone that has the experience. It's why Agents in Charge are older, in their forties or fifties. They have that experience. They know what to expect, what to look out for, how to respond when a situation is presented to them. I didn't have that experience and that lack of experience could get someone killed in the field.

"Fuck," I said, and let out a sigh, running my fingers through my hair.

I climbed off the picnic table and jogged back over to my truck. Koda was instantly poking me with his nose and I reached over to give him some love as I slid into my seat.

"What am I gonna do, Boy?"

Koda whined and pressed his nose into my neck. I wrapped my arms around him and took comfort in his soft fur. Koda always knew when I needed a hug or some love. He was very attuned to my emotions and that was something I relied on more and more, lately. After a moment I pulled back and spoke.

"We gotta go see Roland. He's not going to be happy about this."

I already knew that Roland wasn't going to like that I would be going after Monroe. Even more so, that he couldn't help.

He had to keep an eye on Tyler. He needed to make sure Tyler was safe and I knew he was the best man for the job. He was in love with Tyler and that meant there was no one better to protect him.

I wasn't certain if Monroe would go after Tyler again or not. It would be smarter for him to get the hell out of the country, but I also knew that wasn't going to be simple for him. Chances were, he was on the run and getting as far away from the State as possible. It wasn't going to be a simple and easy find.

He was a cop.

Had been a cop for a long time.

He had an escape plan and he was days ahead of us.

I put my truck in gear and headed back to town. I needed to update Roland and let him know what was going on. Then, I would need to find a motel room to stay in until I could find my own place.

MASON

I knew I could stay with Roland and Tyler, but I needed my own space. I needed a spot where I could be alone and not have to put on a show for anyone. My life was changing once again, and I wasn't sure how I felt about any of it.

CHAPTER EIGHT

Mason

"ANY UPDATES?" I asked Roland as I handed him a coffee.

Tyler was still being kept in the hospital to help him heal from all of the smoke he inhaled. I knew from personal experience it wasn't good to breathe in that much smoke, and for a person with asthma like Tyler had, it'd be far worse.

I still couldn't believe when we had arrived at the bar that it was up in flames that badly. My heart went straight to my throat when Koda ran right into the blazing inferno. His paws were going to be a bit sore from the heat of the fire, and the scare had taken years off of my life, but thankfully, he was okay.

"The doc isn't going to give him any more sedation. He thinks it'll be okay for him to wake up today and then he'll pull the tube out."

"Good. That's good, Roland."

"Is Koda okay?" he asked, concern lacing his features.

Leave it to my brother to be concerned for my dog. I smiled, touched at his troubled state. He loved Koda, too, and it showed.

"He's good. A doctor checked him over

for me and put some cream on the bottom of his paws. First degree burns, but in a few days he'll be okay. I've got his paws wrapped to keep him from getting any dirt in and aggravating his burns. He's hanging out in the kid's playroom, right now, on the floor."

"You left him there?" he asked, clearly confused. Not that I could blame him, Koda went everywhere with me.

When I'd arrived at the hospital, I'd immediately headed to where the children from yesterday were being held. They were all being kept to ensure they didn't have any problems from the drugs they'd been breathing in. When I got there, that cop, Jarod, was there with Isaiah, a social worker. They were making sure the kids were okay and well taken care of. I knew Isaiah would have his hands full with trying to get the kids placed in safe foster homes. It was just another reminder that I would have to help them overhaul the foster system in town. It was going to be a lot of work.

"Jarod was there with the kids as Isaiah worked with one of the doctors. I called Koda to come when I was ready to leave, but he didn't want to follow. Apparently, he's happy to lay next to Jarod."

"Maybe Koda finally sniffed out your soulmate." Roland couldn't help but chuckle at that.

I rolled my eyes at him and made sure he knew it. I didn't believe in soulmates. That was just some bullshit that Hallmark put out into the world to make people keep chasing after people.

To seek out romance so they could try

and find their soulmate.

Deep and meaningful connections were pointless.

Dating was pointless.

Everyone was either fake and hiding their true self, or they cheated. It was better to stick with having a one-night stand. No emotions were involved and both parties got what they wanted.

It was just that simple.

Besides, Jarod wasn't my type. I liked the spinners, the ones that were small and easy to toss around a room. I didn't bottom and I was not interested in some top trying to convince me I should.

Who says Jarod is even gay?

He didn't come across as gay. I knew I didn't, either, but people knew I was gay. It wasn't something that I was interested in hiding. I saw what happened with

Roland when he tried to hide it. He lost the love of his life to a drunk driver all from a fight about him coming out. It wasn't worth all of that heartache to hide who you were.

"What do we know?" Roland asked, moving our attention back to what mattered the most.

"Well, the tests have started to come back and it's looking like all the kids are addicted to cocaine. The doc is going to keep them for at least a week, possibly two, depending on how bad the withdrawals are. Dana has lawyered up. Apparently, she expected Jasper to come back and rescue her. Once she figured out he left her holding the bag, she clammed right up and yelled lawyer. I'm trying to get her denied bail, but I don't know if it'll stick. We have all of the electronics from the house and more than enough evidence of the drugs. But we still can't find him. None of the kids are talking about it. The few that have talked, all said it was Dana, that Jasper didn't even know about the drugs."

I had managed to get an update on everything that had been going on with the case. It was a lot to try and manage, because we had to make sure Dana also went down for the crimes that happened in the house.

"Bullshit. It was in his basement. Of course he knew about the drugs. He's trained them to put all of the blame on his wife. Like a fucking coward."

Of course he did. That is exactly what a coward does. He had it all figured out. He knew how to make it appear like it was all Dana and not the dedicated and highly decorated cop. He was smart and it was going to take a good amount of work to try and find him. We would, but I didn't know how long it would take.

"I got a BOLO out on his ID and his photo is being sent to every federal agency all across the country. I'll find him, but it might take some time. I've been put in charge of the task force that is going to be dedicated to finding Jasper."

There was more to it than that, but we didn't need to get into everything, right now. Roland had enough on his plate to worry about. He didn't need this to go with it.

"Once Ty is set back home, I can help you with finding Jasper."

"You're not on the task force, Roland."

He wasn't going to like that fact, and I knew he was going to snap at me over it. I couldn't blame him. If I ever loved someone like he loved Tyler, I would have been pissed and looking for blood. He wasn't going to like it, but there was nothing he could say to change my mind. He was too close to it and he needed to stay with Tyler to help him recover and to make sure he was safe.

"What the fuck are you talking about?" Roland snapped, as expected.

"You can't be out there looking for Jasper. I know you want to, I get it, but if you are out there with me, who the hell is going to be protecting Tyler? The only way to make a case against Jasper for multiple counts of murder and child trafficking is Tyler's testimony. Jasper knows that and he won't stop until Tyler is dead. You need to be with him, protecting him."

I could tell he wasn't happy about it, but he could also understand where I was coming from. He let out a sigh and gave a small nod in defeat. I went and put a comforting hand on his shoulder as I spoke.

"I'll get him, I promise you."

"I know."

Roland's faith in me was unwavering and that only added to the pressure I was already feeling. The last thing I wanted to do was to let him down. I was afraid, though, that I already had before this thing even started.

"I'm going to grab my stuff from your place and grab a motel room, for now."

"No, Mase, you can stay with me," Roland instantly said.

"I know, but it'll be easier for me to stay at a motel. I'll be working late and you will be busy keeping Tyler safe. The Government pays for it, anyway, so it's not like I'm out money. I'm gonna get going. I have a lot of work to prep."

I needed to start to figure out who I was going to bring onto the task force and who would be able to pick up everything and move to a new town. I wasn't just asking them to come down for a case. This was a permanent move. That wasn't easy. I would need to find people that were skilled and would be willing to relocate. It was going to be a lot of work and I wasn't sure if I was truly ready for it, but I hadn't been given any choice. I would run this task force the best that I could. I just hoped it would be good enough.

CHAPTER NINE

Jarod

WALKING INTO THE station today felt different than it had yesterday.

I didn't feel different, though. Well, I felt sore from the punch I took. I woke up this morning to one very nasty looking bruise along the right side of my jaw line. I had taken some over the counter meds and I was hoping they would kick in soon.

The atmosphere was what felt different in the station.

Normally, when I walked in, you could hear chatter or someone laughing. Things were kept pretty light and carefree. We didn't catch darker cases. There were no homicides or sexual assaults that sucked the life out of you. Today, though, there was no talking, no soft chuckles. There was nothing but silence. The energy in the room was tense and filled with unease. It was as if everyone was afraid to say the wrong thing so they were all opting for this awkward silence.

It was uncomfortable.

I made my way over to my desk as quietly as humanly possible. I didn't want to attract any attention, because I knew the tension would be taken out on me.

It normally was.

The second I sat down, Baxter was instantly on me. He was not in a good mood. I could clearly see it all over his face. He was still pissed off at me for my comment yesterday about Monroe. I shouldn't have said it, but the words were out before I could even stop them.

It didn't happen often, but when it did I always regretted it. I was, normally, pretty good at not saying things out loud. I had a great inside voice, but every now and then, I used my outside voice and typically it resulted in a punch.

"You are late on Rasp's paperwork. You were supposed to have that in yesterday," Baxter said with a tough edge to his voice.

Typically, I had to do everyone's paperwork. That was a rookie's job, according to over half of the police force.

The only ones that didn't have me doing their paperwork were Detective Hollingsworth and Detective Wright. It didn't matter how many months I had on the job. It didn't matter how many cases I'd closed. All that mattered to them was that I was the newest detective, so I would always be the rookie. Even if another officer was promoted to detective, I would still be the punching bag because I was the opposite of everyone here.

"I'm sorry, I was pulled in for the raid and then, I was working the crime scene and talking to the victims."

"That's not your job. You don't get to work crime scenes or talk to any victims or suspects. Your job is to do paperwork until you have proven that you are not a useless idiot. And until you can manage to get paperwork in on time, you will never be out in the field again. You're the most worthless and useless rookie I have ever had to put up with. The day you get kicked out of here, the better this town will be." Baxter headed off and I could see that everyone was staring at us.

I could see the disgust in their eyes. Baxter obviously had told them what I had said in the basement and the blue wall was in full effect. I was going to be going through hell, now more than ever, because I dared to say something about a highly decorated detective.

These next few months were going to be brutal.

I grabbed Rasp's folder that contained the paperwork that was now past due and got to work on it. I was going to have to stay late tonight if I wanted to get all of this done.

CHAPTER TEN

Jarod

I WAS ONLY an hour into my work when Captain Perry came out into the bullpen. We all gave him our attention as we heard him coming our way.

Captain Perry had a heavy walk. You could hear him coming and there was no mistaking it. I was hoping he had an update on the case.

"I need you all to work on clearing out the small conference room. Agent Wright has been cleared to put together a task force with federal agents and local police to go after Monroe. The task force needs a place to work. I would appreciate it cleared out quickly. They should be here shortly."

A task force?

This was a huge opportunity. An opportunity I had been waiting for. I had been offering my skills to other police departments in nearby towns, but a task force that had the ability to hunt down Monroe, no matter where in the country he was located, it was a huge opportunity. It wasn't just an opportunity for me, but any detective here that had wanted to move up in rank. A task force opened so many doors. It could be a career changer for anyone that got to be on it.

"Will any of us get to be on it?" Detective Hollingsworth asked.

"That is up to Agent Wright. It's his task force and his call. I will supply him with files for detectives that I think would be helpful to him. It's up to him, in the end."

I had to talk to Captain Perry to see if I could be one of those detectives he handed over to Agent Wright. I knew I was on the low end for experience, and I literally had no seniority, but I had a great solve rate.

I would have an even higher one if the other detectives who I'd helped to solve their cases allowed me to put my name on the case. Even the detectives that I helped in other stations—they'd let me work the case, but they always took credit for the arrests.

It had never bothered me before. I wasn't in it for the spotlight in the newspaper or the "atta boy" that followed. I wanted to help people, to protect them. Solving a case was all that mattered to me. Getting the bad guy was all that mattered to me.

Now, though, I was hoping it wouldn't hurt my chances of getting onto this task force. I couldn't be a federal agent or go to a major city, so working on this task force might be my only chance at experiencing true police work. I couldn't let this opportunity pass me by.

We all got moving and I approached Captain Perry. I needed to speak with him for a quick moment before he started to go through the files he wanted to hand over.

"Captain Perry, could I speak with you for a moment?"

"Of course. What would you like to discuss?" he asked as he guided me over to a more quiet area in the bullpen.

"I wanted to talk to you about my file being an option for the task force."

Captain Perry gave me a small nod and I could tell by the blank look on his face that I wasn't going to like this. He always got that look when he was about to give someone news they didn't necessarily want to hear.

"I appreciate your enthusiasm, Lopez. However, I'm only handing over files for veteran detectives with extensive field experience and a high solve rate. You don't have the type of experience that the task force is in need of to catch Monroe. They need guys that can hit the ground running without having to train or explain things. You're a good detective, Lopez, but you aren't ready for something as serious as the task force."

The only thing that hurt more than not being selected, was being told by your Captain that you weren't good enough to even be considered.

That stung, and it stung hard.

It took everything in me to school my features and not let that pain show through. I was good at my job. At least, I thought I was, but now, I was starting to doubt it. I knew that my name was often kept off of the arrest reports. But I thought that *he* at least saw me. I thought that my own Captain noticed the hard work that I put in. That he noticed the long hours I worked. That he noticed me volunteering my time at other police stations. I thought he saw me. I thought he saw my potential and my hard work, but apparently I was completely unnoticeable.

Maybe Baxter was right.

Maybe I was useless.

"Of course. I understand, Captain," I said, maintaining a neutral voice.

He gave me a warm smile before he headed off.

I sucked in a shaky breath and did my best to make it seem like I was not upset. Being upset in this station, around these men, it wasn't a good idea.

I went to start to help clear out the room, but I didn't even make it outside of the bullpen when Baxter was back, and based on the pleased look on his face, he knew what had just happened between Captain Perry and me.

"You actually thought a little shit like yourself would be placed on an elite task force?" Baxter said with a chuckle.

"You are nowhere good enough for something like that. You will never be good enough. The only reason you even got promoted to detective was because the force needed to be more diverse and you are one of the few legal Latino's in the country. Give it up, Rookie, you will never be good enough for anything more than filling out paperwork. And you can't even do that right," Baxter said as he walked by me, making a point of hitting his shoulder against mine, pushing me back into the wall slightly.

Today was not going so well.

It was bad enough I already felt like crap after being hit by someone that was supposed to be my partner, but I just got smacked down by my Captain. I discovered that my own Captain didn't think I was capable of doing more on this job.

That I wasn't good enough.

Baxter's words only twisted the knife in further.

I turned and headed outside. I needed some air. I needed time to get my thoughts and emotions back under lock and key. I couldn't be around these guys today until I did.

The second I walked outside, I took a deep breath in to try and get the hurt out of my system. I knew it wasn't that simple. It was going to haunt me for the rest of the day.

Hell, for most of the week, most likely.

Still, I was used to the abusive words. I was used to having to keep all of my emotions and facial expressions in check. I had done this for the majority of my life and I would keep doing it until the day came when I could finally be myself with someone. When I could finally trust someone on a deep level that would allow me to be vulnerable with them. I doubted that person would ever be in my life, though. Even if they liked me, I knew if they knew who my parents were, it would all be over.

I was pulled out of my thoughts when three cars and a truck pulled up. I instantly noticed Koda in the front seat of the truck and Agent Wright in the driver's seat.

I couldn't help but notice how sexy he looked.

He was wearing all black, once again, and I wanted nothing more than to run my hands all down his chest. I would bet my entire paycheck that he looked remarkable underneath his clothes.

Agent Wright got out of his truck and Koda jumped down from the driver's side. Koda bounded over to me and I bent down so I could give him some love.

"Hey Boy, how are you feeling?"

"Detective Lopez, right?" Wright asked me as he walked over to us.

"Yes, Sir," I answered, before I stood. I went back to petting Koda's head as he insistently nuzzled my thigh.

"You can drop the Sir. And Koda is doing good. His paws are healing great. Did you get any more out of those boys?"

"No, they wouldn't talk. They're too afraid to go against Monroe. I suspect that Monroe threatened the other children if any of them spoke."

"That's normally the case. Even if they did say Monroe was there at the house, and was the ringleader, we could never get them to testify. Even if they agreed, I couldn't in good conscience allow them to. It would be too dangerous for them. We'll find Monroe another way."

He sounded so confident and I couldn't help but wonder how many times he'd done this before.

How many criminals did he hunt down without any evidence or leads?

He worked for Homeland Security, but I didn't know what exactly he did there.

"Do you hunt down a lot of criminals like Monroe?" I couldn't help but ask.

"I work for the Special Victims Unit. I go after criminals that commit crimes against children. So yeah, I go after guys like Monroe every day." He gave me a small professional smile before he continued.

"I gotta get my guys in there and brief them. I'll see ya around."

"Yeah, of course. Good luck," I said slightly awkwardly.

I desperately wanted to be one of the guys that got to help, but I knew that was never going to happen, unfortunately. I was a paper pusher, and it looked like that was all I would ever be in this station.

CHAPTER ELEVEN

Mason

I WAS DRAGGING my ass this morning.

Today was the day my guys would be coming in and I would need to get them all caught up on Monroe and everything that they were signing on for. I didn't inform them before hand that this could be a permanent placement. I wanted to get guys here to help me find Monroe and then, if they wanted to stick around that would be great.

I knew I was supposed to be building a task force, but I couldn't do that, right now. At least, not fully. I had to focus on getting Monroe.

I had reached out to Isaiah and he had agreed to be on the task force as a social worker. He also recommended his colleague and friend, Travis Manning.

I now had two social workers and three temporary guys. I also knew that Captain Perry was going to be pulling some files of his best and most veteran detectives for me to go through and pick who I wanted to be on the task force.

I knew I had to have a local detective or a couple of them, but my issue with that was the fact that Monroe came from this station. I knew that didn't mean they were all bad. I understood that there were bad apples in every good bunch, but I couldn't help but question how many bad apples there were in this station. I couldn't go off of the files alone. I had to ask Roland about some of them and see what he thought.

Task forces were generally built to catch as many criminals as possible. That didn't always translate to veteran feds or detectives. You had to put a group of people together that all brought something unique to the table, but something that the task force needed to make them more efficient. Having over a hundred years of experience on a task force didn't always work. Having too many people that believed their way was the best didn't work and that was what you typically had when you got a group of veteran detectives in the joint.

It was going to be a fine line I would have to walk, and to try and figure out how to best maneuver with Captain Perry. We would be operating out of his station, at least until we had received some funds to make our own station, but that wouldn't be until we could prove ourselves and that started with this case.

After saying good morning to Jarod, who was sporting a new bruise to the side of his face, I strolled into the precinct. I'd wanted to ask him about it, but it wasn't any of my business, despite how it pissed me off to see it.

Koda was screwing with me, too.

Koda never acted that way to a stranger. He'd never stayed with someone else, especially after I called him to come. I couldn't help but wonder what he was picking up that I was missing. And, of course, now, I couldn't stop thinking about the milk chocolate-skinned man with soulful brown eyes. He wasn't my type.

He was the opposite of my type, in fact, so then why couldn't I get him out of my head?

"Agent Wright, I see you have brought some men with you today," Captain Perry said as we walked in.

"Captain Perry, yes, I have brought some guys from my neck of the woods, specialized federal agents to help find Monroe. Do we have a spot we can work from?"

"I have the small conference room being cleared out for you. Should only take another moment. If you come with me to my office, I'll hand you those files."

I simply gave a nod and followed the Captain down the hallway. I knew the guys would stay there until I came back and I could show them where we would be setting up shop. This was nothing new to them. We had never all worked together before, though, and I was expecting a shitshow until everyone settled in.

I closed the door to Captain Perry's office behind me. He immediately went over to his desk and grabbed what looked like ten files. He spoke as he handed them to me.

"These are the more experienced detectives I have. They have over twenty plus years each and their track records are impressive."

"Thanks, I'll review them. Where's Hollingsworth?"

I didn't know who I could trust within

the station, but I did know I could trust Roland. He told me that Hollingsworth would be an asset. He only had five years on the job, he hadn't joined until he was twenty-two, but before that he was in the air force and I had a huge respect for veterans. I knew they could handle themselves out in the field and they saw things differently. They were trained to see small reactions within people, to sense their surroundings. It was a huge asset to have out in the field. Not only that, Roland trusted him and Roland had vouched for him, so I knew I could trust him and that meant more to me and my gut instincts than any experience written on a piece of paper.

"Oh, he's not what you are looking for. He's only been on the job for five years and only a detective for one. He doesn't have the experience that someone would need for this type of work."

"Experience isn't everything, Captain. Right now, it's about who I can trust to follow orders and do what it takes to help me find Monroe. Now, I don't *need* to include anyone in the station, but we are working out of here and we are supposed to be working together on this task force, so I would like to have a couple of detectives. Who I pick, though, is up to me and Ro says I can trust Hollingsworth."

"Ro?" Captain Perry asked with a smirk.

"I couldn't pronounce his name when I was younger so I called Roland *Ro* and it's always stuck. I usually try to remember to use his full name when in company but occasionally it slips. Where's

Hollingsworth?" I wasn't in the mood to go down memory lane, right now. I needed to get everyone caught up so we could get going on this manhunt.

"He's here today. He'll be in the bullpen. Will Roland be on the task force?"

"Not for this case. The Governor is looking to make this team permanent if it works out. If that happens, then he will be on the task force. For now, he needs to be close to Tyler in case Monroe goes after him. The other kids aren't talking, which means the only witness that can testify is Tyler. He needs to be protected until we get Monroe in custody."

"Understandable. What type of cases will the task force be working on after this?"

I could tell that Captain Perry was very

interested in having the task force here. I couldn't blame him. It would make the station stand out amongst the others in the nearby cities.

"Crimes against children all over the country. It has the potential to be pretty major. Right now, though, we have to focus on finding Monroe before anything else can happen. No one knows that there is a potential for the task force to stick around, not even Roland, so please keep that under wraps. I don't want people to know until it's official."

I was trying to not think about the fact that this task force could be major. I didn't want to get ahead of myself. I didn't want to worry about what could happen after this case. I wasn't ready to lead a task force and I was not telling myself that I was leading a task force. I was running an investigation to find Monroe so the man that Roland loved remained safe and no more children would suffer under that monster's hand.

"That sounds like it will be a huge opportunity, but also has the power to do a lot of good. I hope it gets to continue after this. A lot of children need someone like you looking for them." Captain Perry gave me a small smile before he spoke again.

"Come on, I'll show you where you guys can set up and get Hollingsworth for you."

I gave a nod and we headed out. As we went back to the bullpen, I could see all of the detectives were looking at us and I knew they would be waiting to see if I would be picking them for this task force.

"Hollingsworth, with me," Captain

Perry said.

I could see that everyone was surprised that Captain Perry was calling for Hollingsworth. He didn't have anywhere near the experience level as most of the detectives here, but I didn't care about that.

I could also see that others were assuming that Hollingsworth was going to be the task force bitch and run around doing our grunt work. I wasn't about that, though, not even with my own rookies.

Rookies weren't there to be grunts, they were there to be trained so they could grow and become their own agent that could save more lives. Treating your rookie like a dog didn't help anyone, especially not the innocent people in the world.

Hollingsworth got up and he followed

all of us as we were guided to the little conference room that had been cleared out. It was undersized, but we could make it work. We had worked in smaller places. The room had a table big enough to fit six people, and all along the walls were white boards. We would have enough space to get the files up on the walls and keep everything organized in terms of leads.

"Let me know if you need anything," Captain Perry said to me before he strolled out and closed the door behind him.

I tossed the detective files down on the table as my guys all stood around waiting to see what was going on. I had only told them that I needed help finding someone. I didn't want to have the same conversation over and over again, so I figured I would wait to reveal everything at once.

I did see the file boxes that we had for Monroe were already in the room so we could hit the ground running, at least.

"As you all know, I'm getting a task force up and running to find Jasper Monroe. I'll get into who he is in a moment. But first, I am Supervisory Special Agent Mason Wright. I have been with Homeland Security for seven years. I know three languages and I am a K9 handler," I said, before I gave a nod down to Koda as I continued.

"This is Koda. He is five years old and has been my K9 partner since he was eight weeks old. He is trained in attack, scent tracking, bomb detection, and he is good with victims." I then pointed over to Hollingsworth for him to go next.

We needed to get the introductions out of the way so we could focus on finding Monroe. I hated this part, but it was needed so everyone knew something about the person they were standing beside. Trust was huge and you couldn't trust someone that you barely knew.

"Detective Logan Hollingsworth. I'm twenty-seven and have been on the job for five years, one year as a detective. I joined the air force when I was eighteen and was medically discharged when I was twenty-one after a bad plane crash. I can fly any plane or chopper, and I have no idea why I'm here." Hollingsworth said, clearly confused why I would select him. I couldn't blame him. He didn't have the experience that most would assume was needed for this.

"You're here because you have the

training from the air force, plus my brother trusts you. He vouched for you and I take that very seriously. It's not always about experience, Hollingsworth, it's about the skills that you bring to the table. I got no problem training. I got a problem not being able to trust someone. That's why you're here."

"I won't break that trust," Hollingsworth promised.

"I'm Cooper Jones, but everyone calls me Coop. I'm twenty-nine and have been a Fed since I was eighteen. I'm a hacker and analyst. I work for Homeland Security for the Counter Terrorism department. There isn't anything I can't hack. I've been doing it since I was seven years old."

"So, you're a hacker prodigy?" Hollingsworth asked.

"Let's just say, be happy that I work

for the good guys," Cooper said with a wink.

"I'm Special Agent Rafe Dallas. I'm thirty-five and have been working for the Department of Justice for five years. Previously, I was a Navy SEAL. I run investigations into dirty feds and get them prosecuted. I specialize in hand to hand combat and tactical."

"I'm Ryzen, people call me Ry. I'm thirty and a sniper."

That was all he was going to give us?

I wasn't sure about Ryzen. Rafe and Coop, I knew I could count on and trust. I knew they would be huge assets to helping me find Monroe. Ryzen though, he was a wild card and, normally, I wouldn't be interested in a wild card, but he came highly recommended. His file didn't have a specific loyalty that set claim to him. He didn't work for anyone, but he did work for everyone. Whenever the FBI needed a sniper, they went to him. Whenever NCIS needed a sniper, they went to him. Whenever Homeland Security needed a sniper, they went to him. It was weird, because, as a rule, people didn't float around. He was a Fed, I knew that for a fact, but I couldn't find the agency that was laying claim to him. He also had no last name, not even in his file. There was nothing on this guy in terms of personal information. I was starting to suspect he was CIA, but he would never tell me if he was. Because he couldn't.

"That's it?" Rafe asked, annoyed and confused.

"You wanna know my favorite color?" Ryzen snarked.

"Now that we all know each other, we can get started," I said, shutting it down before it could go any further. I didn't need a pissing contest.

"Jasper Monroe was a detective in this station for almost thirty years. For close to twenty of them, he has been a foster parent, along with his wife, Dana. My older brother, Roland, his new boyfriend, Tyler, was one of those foster kids that lived with them. A few days ago, Tyler gave his testimony against Monroe. Monroe and Dana have been using their foster kids to cook cocaine, package it and deliver it to their dealers in other towns nearby. Monroe has killed some of the foster kids that were either too sick from the drugs or were bringing too much attention to their operation. He has also sold kids to the sex trade when he felt like it. It had been going on for twenty years and, at this time, we have no idea how many were sold and how many have been killed. We don't know where the bodies are buried, either."

"Jesus, fuck. They both in the wind?" Rafe asked, clearly pissed that someone who was supposed to be keeping children safe was hurting them.

"When we did the raid Dana was there, along with their current foster children. Nine of them. We have the drugs and we have Dana, but Monroe disappeared a couple days ago. Dana won't give anything up. Claims she had no idea it was even in the house. She is sitting in jail and we were able to get bail denied. She believes that Monroe will come back for her. The children, they all say the same thing: that Monroe is a good man and he didn't know what Dana was making them do. We have tried to talk to the kids, but they are too scared to go against Monroe. It's on us to find him."

"Monroe also set fire to the bar that Tyler works at. He tried to kill him before he skipped town. Thankfully, Tyler is fine and going to make a full recovery. But if Monroe gets wind of Tyler surviving, we believe he will try and have him killed again. We don't have very many dangerous criminals in town, but Monroe has been a cop for a long time. He could have any number of connections to the underground that could come and kill Tyler. Without Tyler's testimony, it would be hard, if not impossible to convict him," Hollingsworth added.

"He couldn't have gotten that far if he's only a couple days ahead of us," Cooper stated.

"This the case files?" Ryzen asked as he kicked the box on the floor.

"That's everything we have. Let's get the intel out and set up. We need to find him before he disappears for good. Or worse, he takes another set of kids."

I wasn't certain what Monroe would do. He was used to having all of this money and now, he would be limited to what cash he had been able to take out or store. We had no idea how much money he had, but a man like him wouldn't be happy if he had to save and scrape by. He would want to get his empire back up and running and in order to do that, he would need to have kids. He couldn't be a foster parent any longer, but that didn't mean he couldn't get kids. There were plenty all over the country who were homeless or in foster homes that wouldn't report them missing.

Monroe would likely have endless connections with the men he associated with. It wouldn't take much to get himself back up and running and we needed to catch him before he did.

CHAPTER TWELVE

Jarod

IT HAD BEEN three days since the task force had started working out of the station.

It hurt a great deal when I discovered that Hollingsworth was singled out for the task force. He had less experience than I did, and yet, he was chosen. I didn't know why he was selected over me, but I suspected it had to do with how close he was with Detective Wright. The two of them had been working a lot of cases together and you could tell they were friends.

Detective Wright had taken Hollingsworth under his wing from the moment he came into the station. I knew they were both veterans and I suspected that old veteran connection was still strong within them.

Everyone else, though, they were also pissed off.

They were clearly jealous and they were not afraid to hide it.

They all believed that Hollingsworth was the task force bitch and was doing all of the grunt work, including bringing them coffee. I had never seen Hollingsworth doing that, but I was also keeping my head down and working so I wouldn't have to make eye contact with anyone. If I made eye contact, I was opening myself up to be berated once again. There was only so much one man could take and I was reaching my limit.

It was a dangerous place for me to be in, because I didn't want to lose this job. I just had to grin and bear it and hope that once everything with Monroe was finished it would blow over and I could go back to being out on the street. As it stood, I could barely leave my desk to take a leak.

Today, my morning was going to be extra special, because I needed to stop in and visit my mother. My mother was a lovely woman. At least, that is what I was told.

Growing up, my parents were all about themselves. They loved each other and they loved spending time together. When my mother got pregnant, it wasn't in their plans, but they had me anyway. They weren't abusive, but they weren't loving, either. Most of the time, they could go all week without saying a single word to me. We would have dinner and I would sit all alone at the table while they were off eating outside on the deck. I was more like a house cat. I could co-exist with them, but I couldn't interact with them. I couldn't destroy their perfect bubble of love they shared for each other.

I had made peace with it a long time ago, that I wasn't important to them. That they didn't want me, but they were going to keep me alive until I was eighteen and could legally leave. It was fair, and I didn't ask for more than I knew they wouldn't be able to give me in terms of love.

MASON

I made sure when I was hurt or sick that I took care of myself, unless there was something I needed an adult to do. I was always afraid that if I bugged them too much, they would leave me somewhere and that was the last thing I wanted.

For the first fifteen years of my life, everything was fine. It wasn't what society would dictate was an acceptable environment for a child to grow up in, but I was surviving. I was getting good grades. I had three meals a day. I was never abused or went without basic needs. I was fine. And then, Special Agent Morgan Torres with the FBI showed up at our front door with an arrest warrant for my father.

As it turned out, my father had been killing women for close to twenty years.

He was a serial killer.

We didn't want to believe it, at first, but then they found his trophies in the basement. There had been a hidden room behind a work shelf that held a photo of each of his victims and a lock of their hair. They were all in plastic ziploc bags and dated.

It was earth shattering and it destroyed my mother and her world. She never wanted to believe it. She believed that someone else had done those crimes. That someone must have broken into the house and planted the evidence.

It was ridiculous and no one believed it.

He was serving five life sentences in a maximum-security federal prison.

It was why I couldn't be a Fed or a cop in a bigger city. If people knew I was the son of a serial killer, one that killed close to a hundred women, they would assume I was a killer, too. I had to stay in a smaller town and do what I could for the people in it.

That was the only way I was going to be able to help people.

After my father had been convicted and sentenced, my mother lost it. It didn't matter that she still had me. I wasn't worth anything to her. She didn't love me, and even if she cared a little, it was definitely nowhere near the amount she loved my father. She started to use drugs, heroin, and before I even knew it, my mother was a full-blown addict.

For the next two years that I was at the house, we made it work. I would clean and cook and make sure she was taken care of. It didn't matter that she was the parent. I knew she couldn't do it. So, I took on the responsibilities. I made sure the bills were paid, I made sure my homework was done, that we had food, and that my mother ate three times a day. I would transfer money from her bank account into my own so I could make sure she didn't spend it all on drugs.

When I left at eighteen to go into the police academy, my mother went downhill and she hasn't stopped. When the mortgage for the house was too high, she sold it and moved into an apartment. When the rent for the apartment was too high, she moved into a rundown piece of shit place. All so she could spend more money on drugs.

For the past seven years, I had been trying to help her without enabling her. When she didn't have any food, I would buy her groceries. When she was behind on rent, I would cover it by paying her landlord directly. I knew it wasn't helping her to get sober, but I was terrified that she would die because she didn't have food in her fridge or a place to sleep at night.

I had paid to put her through three rehab centers for treatment, each one failed to keep her sober for more than thirty days. Two years ago, I had to pay off her debt to her drug dealer after he beat her into a coma for being behind ten grand. Between the rehabs and her debt, I was tapped out in savings.

Ever since being back in town after the Police Academy, I'd been going by every couple of weeks to check in on her. I hated going there, but I felt like I was responsible for her. It was because of my father that she was the way she was, and even though it wasn't my fault, I still felt responsible for her.

Walking into her apartment, I was immediately hit by the smell of old food and drugs. She lived in a rundown apartment building on the Southside of town. The building itself was very old and everyone that lived here were either junkies or prostitutes. My mother currently lived alone, but she was often with other people at the apartment. Almost like a flop house. The rent was cheap and I was fairly certain she was paying some of it on her back to the current landlord.

I knew she was prostituting and I hated it, but I couldn't fix her. I wished I could, but she was the only one that could make that choice. I had tried for years to get her to choose a healthier lifestyle, to decide on getting sober, but she just wouldn't.

"Hi, Mom," I said as I walked over to the small kitchen with the couple of bags of groceries I bought for her.

She was sitting on the couch and high, but I could tell she hadn't just done it so she was more lucid. Sometimes, that was worse than when she was passed out from it. If she was lucid, she was talking and, sometimes, what she said was not something I wanted to hear. Today was already going to be bad enough with having to be at the station and around everyone. I didn't want to add more abuse to my day.

"What are you doing here?" she said with a slight disgust to her voice. Apparently, she was in a mean mood.

"I'm bringing you some food," I simply said, making sure to keep my voice calm.

"I don't need your fucking charity."

"It's not charity, Mom. I just want to make sure you are eating properly," I said as I started to put things away. She wasn't in the mood for company, at least, not my company, so the sooner I got out of there the better.

"You want to do something for me? I could use a couple hundred bucks."

I bet she could. She needed her next fix just like she always did. Ever since she started to use it, she was always looking for her next fix. I had no idea who had introduced her to heroin, but from the moment she first injected it into her vein she was hooked. There was no going back from it and I had to watch her slowly deteriorate in front of me.

"You know I won't give you money for drugs."

"What good are you, then? I got stuck with a worthless son, who can't even give his mother what she needs. You've always been worthless, always crying when you were younger. All you do is take from me. You took everything from me. The least you could do for your mother is make sure she has cash on her."

I don't know why she seemed to think I was always crying growing up, unless she was referring to when I was an infant. She always made it seem like I was annoying and took everything from her when I was younger but that couldn't be further from the truth. I kept to myself. I made sure I didn't ask them for any help unless I had no choice to. I don't know why she felt like I had taken her life from her.

"If you weren't doing drugs it would be a different story. I can't support your decision to get high, Mom."

This had been a conversation we have had before. She knew I wouldn't support her drug addiction. I suppose I was supporting it by bringing her groceries and helping to pay her rent when she couldn't cover it. I had also paid off her previous debt to her dealer when she was almost killed. Some could call me an enabler, but I refused to give her cash. I knew she would only use it to purchase heroin.

I had tried to get her sober many times, but she didn't want it. She wanted this life. I don't know why she wanted it, but she wasn't interested in getting healthy and making something of herself for the rest of the life she had to live.

"Then get the hell out! You're worthless to me. I wished you had been killed when I was pregnant. You ruined everything in my life. I hate you!"

I finished putting the two things away before I headed out. I didn't even bother with saying goodbye. It would only fuel more hatred from her. I had heard it all before. She often told me how I was worthless and should never have been born. That she wished I had died.

It wasn't anything new.

Still, it hurt to hear.

I made my way back downstairs and out to my car. I had to get to the station for my shift. As badly as I would have loved to call in sick, I knew it would only make things worse for me tomorrow. I had to suck it up and focus on the work. That was the only way I was going to make it through.

CHAPTER THIRTEEN

Mason

IT WAS NEARING ten o'clock at night when I finally decided to call it a night. At least, at the station. I would be going back to the motel and doing more work.

It had been a week since the task force was put together and, so far, all we had managed to do was not find Monroe. Cooper had been all over Monroe's computer, but there was nothing on it that could link to a location or a person we could reach out to. He had even searched his cell phone and work computer. We had nothing in that sense.

We needed to find something, a place where we could start. A person that we could talk to that we could try and flip to get Monroe's location.

We had shit and it had been a week.

We were all trying our best, I knew we were, but our best wasn't good enough. Not this time around. Too much was riding on us finding Monroe. Roland had already lost one man that he loved. I couldn't be the reason that he lost another.

I had to find Monroe, no matter what.

I made my way back down the hallway to reach the conference room. I was the only one left in the station. Any calls that would come in, not that there would be any, they were forwarded to whoever was on call for the night. There was no reason to pay to have people sitting around all night doing nothing.

Just before I walked into the conference room, I noticed Jarod standing there looking at the evidence board. I didn't even know he was still there. I hadn't paid much attention to the other detectives in the station this past week, but every time I looked into the bullpen, I saw Jarod at his desk, working. It seemed like he always had work to do when everyone else had none. I couldn't help but wonder if maybe he was being bullied because he was new.

"You're working late," I said as I walked in. Koda lifted his head, but just laid right back down. He was in no hurry to get up.

Jarod turned around, a bit startled to see me, even though Koda was still in the room. I suspected he figured he could slip out before I got back from the bathroom

"I was just finishing up some paperwork. Sorry, I didn't mean to invade your space."

"Sure you did, that's why you're standing in it. I don't mind people being inquisitive, and never apologize for being curious, Jarod. You're a detective, it's part of who you are."

I didn't like how he always seemed so unsure of himself. From what Roland had told me, he was smart. He suspected that Jarod was a genius and I was leaning toward agreeing with him.

When you deal with guys that have a

higher IQ, you tend to have to deal with their quirks. They were normally awkward, shy, and a bit weird. They tended to like things done in a certain order, or they always forgot where they put their keys. It was little things, but generally that indicated that they were smarter than the average person.

I like smart people.

I like geniuses, because they don't see the world, they see through the world. It was always an asset to have on a team. I hadn't brought any other detectives onto the task force, yet, because I wasn't sure who I could trust. I didn't know if I could trust Jarod because his partner was Baxter, Monroe's best friend. Jarod could have bad practices or he could believe that the blue wall protects every cop, no matter the crime. He could be a wild card and I already had one with Ryzen. I didn't need another one.

"Yes, Sir. I'll get out of your way," he said, but before he could move I spoke.

"What do you see?"

I moved closer so we could talk normally and for him to not feel like I outranked him. I was a Fed, but I wasn't a cop. We were on the same level, as far as I was concerned. I knew some would think otherwise, but I never got caught up in rank when it came to local police.

"A puzzle. One that is missing a lot of pieces. I see a man that is meticulous, organized. He plans ahead and he has back up plans, should he need them. This man is playing chess when everyone around him thinks they are playing checkers. He has everything linking back to his wife, so he must have an escape plan. He knows police protocols, so he knows he can't fly out of the country, he can't drive across either border. So, he needs a new identity, and I wouldn't be surprised if he already had one stashed away. He probably had a go-bag in the trunk of his car just waiting for when he might have to use it. If it was me, I would have multiple license plates so the car couldn't be tracked on satellites."

I couldn't help the smile.

Fuck, he *was* smart.

He knew more than people were giving him credit for.

I had seen his file. It wasn't that impressive. However, I knew that most rookies didn't get credit for arrests. That they had to earn it, and in a police force this size, there weren't many opportunities for him to earn it.

"Why don't the others like you?"

I could very easily pick up the tension in the bullpen when Jarod was there. They gave him dirty looks, they dropped their files on his desk, they didn't like him, and I needed to know why.

Jarod let out a soft sigh before he spoke.

"I said something to Baxter in Monroe's basement on the night of the raid. He was in denial about everything, even the chemicals being used to make cocaine. I made a comment about them making breath mints instead and he didn't take it too kindly. Even with all of the evidence staring right in their faces, they all want to put their heads in the sand and pretend like it's not happening. When good people do that, the bad people get to keep hurting people and then we become just as bad, if not worse, for standing by and doing nothing to stop it."

"I couldn't agree more. When good people do nothing, the bad people get to keep hurting innocent lives and it's those innocent lives that matter. People need to act when they see something wrong happening. And that is what a cop is supposed to do. No matter who the criminal is. I have to imagine, though, it can't be easy to be the only non-white person in the room."

Jarod was the only person of color in this whole station. For a town that was small and had a problem with gay people, I couldn't imagine they were very friendly with people of color, either.

"I'm Latino, and I don't have an interest in going to bars or strip clubs. It makes it hard to make friends with the white alpha males in the group. Still, I never let it hold me back."

"I don't doubt that."

He didn't come across as someone that took shit lying down. He was strong and he kept showing up to work even when everyone else treated him poorly. He just wanted to help people and it was refreshing. Jarod didn't have an agenda, he wasn't trying to get the highest solve rate so he could be promoted and move on to a bigger city. He was genuinely helping people because he wanted to, because he felt that was his calling.

It was so fucking refreshing.

"You know what I don't see? A cell phone," Jarod said, referring to the case.

"It's right there," I said with a nod to the items on the table in evidence bags. "Coop, our tech guy, he went through it, but there's nothing we could use."

"I'm not talking about that cell phone. Monroe had another one."

"How do you know that?"

We had spoken to everyone who was friends with Monroe, on and off the force. No one had said anything about another phone. There was nothing in his financials that would indicate he had another phone he was paying for. His finances were perfectly clean. There were no cash deposits at all that didn't line up with him working on the force.

Dana, on the other hand, she was a whole other issue. The money they made went into her account and, considering she was a stay-at-home mom, there was no reason for the large deposits.

If Monroe had another phone, not even his closest friends knew about it, so how did Jarod?

"I saw him with it. A couple of weeks before the raid, he was in the bullpen talking with Baxter. He got a text or a call, I can't be sure which, the phone was on silent, but he pulled it out of his pocket, looked at it, and then headed outside."

"It could have easily been his normal phone," I started, but Jarod cut me off.

"It wasn't, it was different. His normal phone is black and shiny, but this phone was black and a matte finish. It was also just slightly a different size and there was no power button on the side. It was on the back. The only phones that have the power button on the back are the LG phones. Monroe always used an iPhone for his personal calls. He used to get pissed off at it when it would randomly decide to update. Not to mention when he got a call on his iPhone, he would take it in the bullpen, but whenever someone called him on the LG phone, he wouldn't answer until he was outside. I just assumed he was cheating on his wife."

See, that right there was why I loved smart people.

Holy fuck, he had another phone and we didn't have it, so either he hid it very well at his place, or he had it with him. That phone had to have all of his contacts for the drugs and maybe even the human traffickers that he dealt with. That phone could lead us to a person that might know where he was, right now.

"That's impressive, Jarod. You are very observant. No one else in the station even knew Monroe had another phone. They never cared to pay attention to the little details. Those details can be what breaks a case. Now, we have to try and trace where he bought it so we can try and find a number."

"I already did. I came in here to put it on the table for you," Jarod said as he pulled out a piece of paper from his pocket.

"I suspected the phone was a burner, because I thought he was cheating on his wife. Having another phone statement would raise a red flag, so I went to the shops in town that sell burner phones, but none of them sold one to him. So, I went to nearby towns and, finally, a shop owner that is an hour away from here recognized Monroe's photo. He paid in cash, but the phones all have to be inventoried for the government, including phone numbers."

I took the offered paper and looked

down at it to see a phone number. Now that we had the phone's number, Coop could try to trace it. Even if he couldn't, he might be able to pull some numbers off of it from the servers.

Jarod was impressive and we needed him.

"Nice work. Your skills are definitely wasted here in a small town like this. But I'm lucky you're here. You start tomorrow, eight in the morning."

"Start what?" he asked, confused.

"You're going to be my partner. You're working the task force."

I could tell that he was shocked. He wasn't expecting to be given the opportunity, even after he worked his ass off to get the phone number for us. He was completely prepared to have to go back to doing paperwork tomorrow morning while we went after Monroe.

I didn't believe in screwing people over. He worked hard to track down this number and I believed that hard work should be rewarded.

"But I don't have the experience," he instantly said when the shock wore off.

"Experience isn't everything. You can't teach someone to have good instincts. You can't teach someone to be smart. That's natural to someone, and I would rather train a person who will grow to be a huge asset than to use someone with twenty years of on the job experience that will contribute nothing."

I could tell he was still feeling unsure about himself. I hated that he felt like he wasn't good enough because he didn't have what other people on the force did. Years of experience meant nothing here and I could tell he had gotten shit for it over the time he'd been a detective. I placed my hands on his biceps as I continued.

"You are incredibly smart. I am willing to bet that you are smarter than you have allowed people to see, because then you would stand out and you don't want to. For whatever reason, you don't want to be noticed and that's fine, until it's not. Until that fear keeps you from helping more people. It doesn't matter what everyone else thinks of you. It doesn't matter what everyone else sees in you. What matters is what you think of yourself. What you see when you look in a mirror. At the end of the day, Jarod, you have to be able to see your reflection and not be disgusted or disappointed in it."

I could see the flood of emotions

flickering through Jarod's eyes. It was as if he had never had someone tell him something like that before. As if no one had ever said anything nice to him. There was a raw pain behind his eyes and I hated seeing it. I hated knowing that someone or multiple someones had been putting him down to the point where he felt so unsure of himself. I could tell he didn't even know what to say to me and I doubted he would be able to say anything at all without his voice catching. I decided to put him out of his misery and change the subject. I spoke as I moved back.

"Come on, let's call it a night, Partner. Koda."

Koda got up and Jarod snapped himself out of it and got moving. We both headed out and I waited to make sure he grabbed his stuff to go home. I didn't want him to sit down and keep working. I didn't care what paperwork he had for someone else to finish, he was mine now, and I was not going to have him too exhausted to function properly.

Once he was ready, we both strolled out into the night and went our separate ways. I was really hoping that Jarod would be able to loosen up and feel more confident in himself as the task force went on.

I also had to ignore the slight warmth that spread throughout my chest and down to my crotch at the thought of having Jarod around me all day. I didn't care what my body said, he wasn't my type and it was just that simple.

CHAPTER FOURTEEN

Jarod

TODAY WAS THE day that I had been waiting seven years for. Today was the day I was going to be a real cop, a real detective. I was going to work on a case that mattered. A case that would save a lot of innocent lives. Innocent children's lives. I was going to get to help the task force bring Monroe to justice.

I knew when everyone in the station found out, they would make it seem like I was just going to be running errands and fetching coffee, but I didn't care. Even if that was what I ended up doing, even if it was grunt work, it would be worth it, because I was still helping them.

Plus, I had given them a huge lead with the phone number that could lead to even more leads that could lead us to Monroe, and it all would have stemmed from that phone number I found. It might be a small role in the larger picture, but I didn't care because I got to help and that was all I wanted.

I walked into the station just before eight, ready to go. The bullpen already had other detectives there, including Baxter. Seeing him normally killed my good mood, but not today.

"Rookie, where's my paperwork?" Baxter demanded as I walked by.

"It's on my desk. You'll have to finish it."

Baxter gave a chuckle as he turned to look at the others in the room before he spoke. "Oh, I'll have to finish it? Paperwork is a rookie's job. You are our bitch and will do whatever the hell it is that we say. Now, get your Mexican ass in your seat and don't move until it's all done."

"I can't. I'm working with the task force. So, all of you will have to do your own paperwork until Monroe is caught."

"Bullshit you're working the task force. They already have a bitch with Hollingsworth, they don't need someone useless like you," Baxter instantly responded.

I could tell none of them were happy about this new piece of information. A good deal of them were bitter that they hadn't been chosen to be on the task force, but Hollingsworth had. It was a blow to their egos that they had been denied the right to be on an elite task force. Now more salt was being poured into the wound by me being selected over them.

"We got a problem here, gentlemen?" Mason said as he walked over to us with a tray of coffees in his hand.

"Nothing that concerns you, Fed," Baxter said.

Mason spoke as he handed me a coffee.

"It does if you are harassing my partner and keeping him from his work."

It warmed my chest to hear Mason

refer to me as his partner. I wasn't sure if he meant it, or if it was just a temporary thing, but it still sounded really good to me.

I had never been called a partner before.

Baxter always called me Rookie or his bitch. Baxter laughed at what Mason said and I knew this wasn't going to end well. There was no way Baxter was going to let me slip away without getting the last word in.

"What part of what I said was funny to you?" Mason asked with an edge to his voice.

"Oh, nothing. I just never figured he worked on his knees. But it does make sense how someone as useless as him got on the task force. I guess liking dick is genetic for you, eh?" Baxter said with a smirk.

Oh, that was going to be bad. I didn't know Agent Wright very well, but I could tell he wasn't impressed by the twitch in his jaw. I knew his brother was gay. I obviously didn't have a problem with it, but I wasn't sure how Mason felt about it. Some guys were cool with their sibling being gay and others were uncomfortable and disgusted by it. I wasn't sure what category Mason would fall under.

"Because I picked an intelligent detective over you, that must mean he only received the position because he lets me bend him over the table to fuck him? It has absolutely nothing to do with the fact that you were useless and hold no value whatsoever to a task force. I'm sure the fact that you failed to notice that your best friend was a drug dealing, child murdering, child sex trafficking asshole doesn't reflect your detective skills, at all. Why don't you do us all a favor and fill out paperwork, seeing as how you couldn't possibly be played by it. I have a task force to run and I need my partner to be all caught up."

Wow... Just, wow.

That moment right there was the best moment of my life.

He actually said that to Baxter. He said it out loud for everyone to hear and he did it without shrinking back or wavering.

God, he was awesome.

Best day ever.

Mason placed his free hand on my back and started to guide me down the hallway, but before we left the bullpen completely, he stopped and turned back to say one more thing.

"Oh, and for the record... yes, I do love dick," he said with complete confidence and the sexiest smirk I had ever seen in my entire life.

Fuck, this man was not only sex on a stick, but he was gay.

He couldn't have been any more perfect.

I had always been attracted to guys like Mason. I liked them bigger and able to defend themselves in a fight. I liked muscles and someone that had no problem being in control and tossing me around. I didn't like it to be violent, but I did like being a bottom and I didn't mind it being a bit rough. It had to be passionate and sometimes passion didn't mean gentle and sweet.

This man was perfect, but he was my

boss, my partner, and that meant we had to keep it professional.

Mason started to move and I had no choice but to move with him. He softly spoke to me as we traveled to the conference room.

"You know, you punch him as hard as you can to his mouth, he'll stop talking shit about you. Or are all of your muscles just for show and you can't fight?" he teased.

"I can fight. I'm just not the type of person to randomly punch someone."

I didn't care for violence and I wasn't one to generally have conflict in my life. My mother was a perfect example of it. It took a lot for me to hit someone without being hit first. Maybe it was my intelligence that made me not see the point in inflicting violence onto someone when you could talk through the conflict. It just wasn't my style.

"I can understand that. But every now and then, assholes need to be punched hard enough to knock some teeth out," he said as we walked into the conference room.

"Who are we punching?" Rafe asked.

"Baxter," Mason answered.

"Oh, fuck, pick me, please," Hollingsworth said as he raised his hand.

I couldn't help the small chuckle at that. Apparently, I wasn't the only one that had been on the wrong end of Baxter. Even Hollingsworth, who was allowed to go out and celebrate with the guys.

"See, he gets it. Every now and then, you gotta just punch the guy to shut him the hell up," Mason said as he placed the coffee down on the table for the guys to grab.

"This is Detective Jarod Lopez. He is our newest member. He was the one who gave us our lead on the cell phone," Mason continued.

"Coop was telling us about it. Nice find," Rafe commented.

"Thanks," I said, slightly awkwardly. I wasn't used to anyone giving me positive reinforcements.

"So as we all figured, the phone was a burner, so I can't put it in Monroe's hands even though we have an eye witness that sold it to him. He could easily say he gave it to someone. I tried to track it, but it's turned off. He most likely bought a new one and dumped this one," Coop started.

"You can't get anything off of it?" Rafe asked.

"I didn't say that," Coop said with a cocky smirk.

"Before, during times of landlines, when you made a call it disappeared the second you hung up. But in the twenty-first century, when you make a call or a text message, it is sent to a satellite that stores the data for forty-eight hours, before it goes to a final server where it remains for thirty days. Now, those servers the general public don't know about. Only computer geeks like myself know they exist, and how to hack into them."

"Legally?" Mason asked.

"Does that matter?" Cooper asked, genuinely confused by the question.

"Not really, just curious," Mason said with a shrug.

Apparently, the need for a warrant to

gain access to secure information was not above him. I wasn't too bothered by it. I knew that the Feds did things a bit differently at times. We were hacking for intel on Monroe, not spying on innocent citizens.

"Naw, it's not legal. But no harm, no foul. I was able to pull the phone numbers that went in and out of the burner phone over the past thirty days. Now, they are all burner phones, but I worked all night building an algorithm that allows me to find cell towers and satellites that picked up those numbers for outgoing calls. I was able to trace where the bulk of the calls were originating from. Columbus, New Mexico," Coop said with a proud smile.

Why would he be calling someone in Columbus, New Mexico?

That made no sense to me. We were nowhere near it. It was a good thirty hour drive. They were on the other side of the country.

How would they be of any help to him while on the run or even before it?

How was he dealing drugs or connecting with child traffickers from all the way out there?

"Alright, Hollingsworth and Lopez, tell us why," Mason said.

I instantly looked at Hollingsworth because I had no idea. I was hoping that maybe he would know, but he looked just as unsure as I did. The trick was, neither one of us wanted to admit it, because the job hadn't really taught us to admit when we didn't know something.

"That was exactly my point. You can't be afraid to ask a question. If you don't know something, then say it. Ask your questions. Voice your opinions. We're all here to catch a criminal and you have to speak up. Hollingsworth, Lopez, no one here is going to ridicule you for asking a question. No one is going to tell you to shut up or make fun if it sounds like a stupid question. There's no such thing as a stupid question. That is how you learn and I would rather teach someone who wants to learn than to deal with an idiot who wants to slide by. Now, with that said, are there any questions?" Mason reassured in a calm voice.

I had never had someone like him in my life. More often than not, if a rookie had a question, they kept their mouth shut and tried to figure it out for themselves.

Mason, though, he had no problems

with people learning and that was refreshing and freeing.

"Why is he communicating with people that are over thirty hours away?" I instantly asked.

"And why would they be communicating with him? If they wanted drugs or children, they could easily get that from the area they are in. Why risk transporting drugs and kidnapped kids across multiple state lines?" Hollingsworth added.

"Look at that, they do know how to ask questions," Rafe said with a smirk.

"Can't answer why, without knowing who," Ryzen answered cryptically.

I didn't know the men in this room outside of Hollingsworth, obviously, but Ryzen seemed very odd. He barely spoke. In fact, this was the first time he had said anything since I arrived this morning. He had a dark aura about him and I could feel how dangerous he was. I didn't know his story, but I couldn't imagine there was a happy one with him.

"Columbus, New Mexico is right on the Mexico border. It is often used as a pit stop for criminal organizations. The town is very small and it's mostly desert and there's no patrol. It's a spot where traffickers can meet to get drugs out of Mexico, get kids and guns going both ways. It's a hot zone and most live in El Paso, which is about an hour up the road," Mason explained.

"So the guys that Monroe called most likely live in El Paso and traveled to Columbus to make the calls, probably while they were already there doing business," I stated.

"Exactly. One of the owners of those phone numbers could get us Monroe. We gotta get to El Paso and start looking into them. I'll make the call for the plane. We're wheels up in two hours," Mason said as he pulled out his cell phone.

"Wheels up? We're going there?" I asked, shocked. I would have figured Mason would have reached out to another Fed to keep looking into it.

"Of course we are. We're running this case. Wherever the leads take us, that's where we go. Pack up. We'll meet at the Baltimore airport in two hours. Pack for at least a week. We don't know how long we'll be gone."

Cooper broke his computer down as everyone else started to head out.

I couldn't help but be shocked. I didn't expect that we would be traveling the country. It was exciting, though. We were actually going to be roaming around and actively looking for Monroe. It felt very official and I was going to remember this for the rest of my life.

With a big smile, I headed out of the conference room and made my way to my car. I had to get home to pack.

I was going on a manhunt.

CHAPTER FIFTEEN

Mason

FLYING WAS NOTHING new to me. Just like flying on a federal jet was nothing new to me. I could tell, though, that it was something special for Jarod. He was like a kid in a candy store the moment he arrived at the airstrip. I couldn't hold it against him. I was like that, too, when I first joined the bureau and got to fly on the private jet that Homeland Security had. It was all very exciting and now, it was just another day to me.

I missed that excitement.

I missed being surprised and full of life at the prospect of a new case. Everything back then was always so new and exciting and now, it was just another day. Another case where I got to experience the horrors this world had in store. That light that I used to see, it was almost too dark to make out now, and I doubted it would ever get bright again.

I mindlessly gave Koda some love, stroking my fingers through his fur as my mind couldn't help but slip back to my conversation with Roland before I headed for Baltimore.

The second Roland opened the door I could tell he had been hoping that I was coming with news for him. I hated that I didn't have anything more actionable for him. Something that would end all of this and he could stop living in fear that one day the man that he loved would be killed. That he would have to lose yet another good man before he had the chance to truly live and love him. I wasn't about to let that happen, but I also knew I couldn't promise that it wouldn't and I hated that. More than anything, I hated that I could be failing my own brother.

"Mase, why are you knocking? You have a key," Roland said, flashing a warm smile as he moved back to let me in.

"Well, I wasn't sure what you and Tyler would be doing. I didn't want to walk in on anything I can't unsee," I teased as I strolled inside.

"Cute, but Tyler still has to heal up

before we have some fun in the bedroom. Or in the kitchen, on the couch, the back deck..." Roland said with a smirk.

"You're an animal, but at least one of us has a chance of getting laid," I retorted as I plopped down on the couch.

"You have plenty of options. Hollingsworth is gay and I also know on the down low that Lopez is, as well. See, he's your soulmate."

"Shut up. I didn't come here for that. Besides, I can't have sex with anyone on my team. That would be unprofessional."

"True, but lots of people do it. Plus, sex is the best way to relieve stress and help people sleep at night. You have not been sleeping. Just because you aren't at the house anymore, doesn't mean I haven't noticed. What's going on with you, Mase?" Roland asked gently, his concern lacing

his voice.

I was not about to tell Roland about what I was diagnosed with. The shrink was a quack, anyway. There was no way I had PTSD. Telling Roland about it would only make him worry and he had enough he needed to worry about with Tyler's safety with Monroe in the wind.

"Nothing is going on. I'm fine."

"Bullshit. Don't give me that crap. We both know that you are not fine. You've been different since you pulled up to my house before this shit show started. Something is going on. What aren't you telling me, Mase?"

This was not a conversation that I was willing to have right now. Hell, it wasn't a conversation that I wanted to ever have. Now was definitely not the time for it. I had to keep my mind focused on Monroe and this case. Afterward, I would have to figure out what I was going to do with my life and how to cope with everything.

"I've brought Lopez onto the task force. He noticed that Monroe was using a different phone than the one we have in evidence. He went all over the nearby towns and was able to track down the store and got a phone number for it. Coop ran it, but it's turned off. He was able to get some phone numbers that were on the phone for the last thirty days. They all originate from Columbus, New Mexico. We're flying out to El Paso within the next two hours to track them down. Hopefully, one of them will have intel on Monroe."

"That's good. I'm glad you picked up Lopez. He's a good detective and he should bring a different viewpoint on the case. Though, I did notice you ignoring my

question. *You have to talk to someone eventually, Mase, before it eats you alive. The job that you do, it's dangerous but it's also soul eating. You can only see the things that you do for so long before it becomes too much. You need to talk to someone. It doesn't have to be me, but talk to someone."*

I hated that I was making him worry. He didn't need to worry about me. I could handle myself. I had been doing this job for seven years and I was fine. I hadn't been shot or stabbed. I had been in fights with taking down a suspect, but that was it. I was lucky. I was one of the lucky ones that hadn't been seriously hurt in the line of duty. I had nothing to have PTSD over. It was stupid and I didn't believe in things that were stupid.

"I'm fine. I just wanted to give you an

update on the case and see how things were around here. Did Tyler remember anything more that we could use, maybe?"

The night that the bar was attacked was all a blur to Tyler. It was from his slight concussion. Memory loss was common. I was hoping he might remember something from that night, because the person that torched the place was quite possibly in the bar when it was open. I knew for a fact that Monroe didn't do it. He was already out of town before the raid went down. He had to have someone else torch the bar to try and kill Tyler. If we could find the perp, it would help prove that Monroe ordered a hit on someone.

"Not yet. He wants to help, but he still has no memories of that night yet. At least, not while he was working. If he does remember something, you will be my first

call. I promise, little brother."

"All right. I have to get going. I still gotta get out stuff from the motel and head to the airstrip in Baltimore. I'll call you later on and check in," I said, as I stood.

Roland stood as well and he pulled me in for a hug.

I instantly wrapped my arms around him and took in the comfort that his embrace always brought me. Even when we were kids, whenever I was scared I always felt better when my big brother wrapped his arms around me. He had a way of making me feel like everything would be okay, even when the whole world was on fire.

Roland didn't pull away, though. He continued to hold onto me until I was ready to let him go. He knew something was wrong and he was allowing me to *have all the comfort that I needed in order to get me through. And it was just another reason why I loved him so damn much.*

"Everything okay?"

I was jarred out of my thoughts by Rafe's voice. He had taken a seat across from me. He had obviously moved while I was lost in the memory. I didn't really know Rafe. I knew of his reputation of being good at his job and that was what I needed. We had never needed to cross paths with him working for the DOJ. He seemed like a good man so far, though.

"I'm good, just thinking about the case. What about you?"

"I'm solid. Hell, I'll go anywhere. I don't care. You just seemed lost in thought for a few minutes, there. Just wanted to check in and make sure you were okay, Boss."

"Naw, I'm fine. You got any family?" I figured I should try and get to know these men a bit better.

"Nope, just myself. This life doesn't really promote stable marriages or relationships. Most people get annoyed when you get called away at a moment's notice. Kinda kills romance and any time off. What about you? You got a boyfriend?"

"How did you know I was gay?" I couldn't help but ask.

"Oh, we all heard you say how you love dick. I figured it wasn't just an expression," he said with a small shrug.

"Nope, I really do."

"Shit, who doesn't?" he said with a smile and I knew right then I wasn't the only one on this plane that preferred men to women.

That was interesting, because according to Roland, both of our detectives were gay as well. Leave it to me to find the few gay men in law enforcement and stick them on a task force. I couldn't help but wonder if Coop would be as well. I doubt Ryzen was, but you never knew. Maybe I would get a clean sweep all across the board.

"Weirdos, mostly. Do you like your position within the DOJ?"

If I was going to make this task force permanent, then I needed to know which of my men would be willing to stick around. If they all wanted to go back to their lives, I would have to start all over again and I wasn't sure how well that would go over. I had chosen each and every single one of these men and I did so with a purpose. If none of them wanted to stick around long term, I wasn't certain I wanted to work with another team. At the same time, I wasn't sure I wanted to be here either, so it wasn't like I could hold it against anyone for wanting to leave after one case.

"It's all right, yeah. Sometimes, I get bored. There's a lot of sitting around and waiting. It's nice being more active again. I miss doing this type of investigation where you have to go from the ground up and build a case. Most of the time, when I get a case file, the legwork is already done for me. I miss getting to do this."

I could understand that. He had been an active Navy SEAL. They didn't do a lot of investigation work, but they did help with the ground level and build up from there. They would focus on the little fish within a terrorist organization and they would work their way up until they got the head of the snake.

"At least you are enjoying the break. Hopefully, we can find Monroe quickly."

"What about the other kids that were killed or sold?"

I had been wondering about that myself. The ones that were killed would be easier to find. There had to be some type of mass grave that Monroe used to hide the bodies. The ones that were sold would be harder. We would have no way of knowing who Monroe sold the children to or where they were taken. They could be dead or they could have been sold and shipped off to another country. We would have no way of tracking them down unless Monroe either admitted to it, which I doubted, or he had some type of ledger that we could use. The harsh reality was, those children would be long gone and we most likely would never find them until it was too late.

"I'm going to see about having someone go looking for the grave. It would have to be close to town, but not in a place that it could be stumbled upon. As for the kids sold, we'll have to see what we can get out of Monroe. Chances are, we'll never be able to find them."

"Yeah, I was afraid of that," Rafe said as he turned to stare out the window.

I knew he was upset.

I couldn't blame him.

This wasn't easy to accept.

He had never had to deal with children in this sense. I was the only one that had to experience the horrors of mankind on a daily basis. The others were used to chasing after criminals that were killers, maybe rapists, but nothing like this. It was hard to handle and I wasn't sure if any of them would be willing to do this for a living.

That wasn't something I had to worry about, right now, though. For now, I had to focus on this case. I was going to find Monroe, no matter what.

CHAPTER SIXTEEN

Mason

WE WENT STRAIGHT to Homeland Security the second we landed.

I had been there before so I easily guided us through the security process and headed up to where visiting agents could work.

We made our way into a conference room that was twice the size of the one at the police station back in Gaithersburg. It would give us all enough room to spread out and work without being on top of each other.

"All right, get set up and start looking into any of the main players in the area. Coop, start trying to track the phone numbers and see if any of them are on or made calls recently. We need someone that we can interrogate to get to Monroe," I said as I placed my bag down.

They all gave a nod and started to spread out and get set up. There were laptops there that they could use, and I knew Cooper had his own rig with him.

I headed back out of the room and moved over to a quieter spot on the floor. I needed to call Roland and check in with him. He answered after two rings.

"Mase, how was the flight?"

"It was fine. We are just getting set up in the conference room, now. Listen, I need to talk to you about something."

"Anything. You know that."

I knew he was expecting me to talk about something personal and not the case, but I wasn't at that point yet, and I doubted I ever would be.

"The children that Monroe sold, they are going to be almost impossible to trace. However, we can find the children that he killed and buried somewhere. Do you think there's anyone in the station that you could trust to find them?"

I could hear the soft sigh that Roland tried to hide. He was disappointed that I hadn't opened up to him, but he would get over it. We were past the age where he could demand that I tell him what was wrong. And I also knew he understood how important it was to give the kids a proper burial. Not to mention, some of them could have families and they deserved to know what happened to their child.

"I don't know about in the station, but I do know two private investigators that stop at nothing to help children. Damien and Sebastian. They'll find the graves and make sure the kids are identified and taken care of. I'll call Damien right now and get him caught up on the cases and he'll start to look for them."

I wasn't sure how I felt about private investigators doing it, but I trusted Roland's judgment. I knew there were some great private investigators in the world.

Ones that did more than just chase cheating spouses.

There had been plenty of times when I was on a case and a private investigator was helping either the local police or an Agency. Some of them were ex-cops or ex-feds that wanted to make a difference in the world without having to conform to the constraints of the law.

"All right, do it. If you think they can be trusted, that is good enough for me. If you could have them focusing on those children, then I'll focus on Monroe. If we can get him alive, we might be able to get him to flip on the men that he sold the other children to."

"Monroe won't do it for free. He'll want some type of deal."

I knew that to be true, but I also knew there wasn't much wiggle room we would be able to give. He was already going to go away for life. The only thing we could give him would be to put him in a lesser prison and put him in protective custody with him being an ex-cop. Other than that, there wasn't much I could do. He had too many federal charges up against him and none of them could be overlooked.

No judge would ever allow it.

"We don't have much wiggle room and he knows it. If he wants to live in prison, though, he'll agree to it. Again, though, that is assuming we will be able to take him alive. He might not let us."

"I know. Just be safe, that's all that I care about," Roland said, and I could hear the deep worry in his voice.

"I'll be fine. Don't worry so much. I gotta get going. The sooner we can track down one of these contacts, the sooner we can, hopefully, get Monroe."

"All right, be safe, and I love you."

"I love you, too, Ro," I said as I ended the call.

I took in a slow and deep breath to calm my anxiety down before I turned and headed back inside the conference room. I had a job to do and I was going to do it.

CHAPTER SEVENTEEN

Mason

"ALL RIGHT, WE have three rooms, so we need to double up. Coop and Hollingsworth, Ry and Rafe," I said as I handed them their room keys.

It was nearing nine o'clock at night when I had decided to call it a day. We all needed to get some sleep or we were going to be useless tomorrow.

We had been able to find one of the contacts in Monroe's burner phone. Jose Vilenti was a major trafficker. From guns, drugs, people. Shit, even exotic animals. If you wanted it, he could get it for you. He was known as a Connector. His job was to put people together and get your product from point A to point B. He worked for a lot of cartels and he made millions a year doing it. He was a major player, and if he dealt with Monroe, that meant that Monroe was a supplier for a cartel.

It was not what I had been expecting. I'd thought Monroe was only a little fish selling children to other little fish. As it was turning out, Monroe was more of a supplier than I thought he was. He was supplying the cartels with kids, but also drugs.

Cartels would use a lot of random

people, men and women, all over the country, to help them generate more money. They would have small time cooks, dealers, kidnappers to produce drugs, sell them, and then send a cut to the cartel. A driver would show up once a month to pick up the cash they were owed and bring it to a cartel stash house. The system was very intricate and it wasn't as simple as taking out one single player. If you wanted to cripple the cartel, you had to take the whole house down. Something that was virtually impossible because any of the higher ups were heavily protected with soldiers, and more often than not, even local police.

"We'll meet back here tomorrow morning at nine to head out to Columbus for the stake out," I added.

We would be heading to Columbus

tomorrow and waiting for the chance to grab Vilenti. With any luck, we'll be able to grab him and I could get intel out of him on Monroe. There were a lot of 'what ifs', but that was what this job was in the beginning of a new investigation.

We all made our way up to our hotel rooms. I was ignoring the fact that I would be sharing a hotel room with Jarod. I didn't like sharing hotel rooms, especially since my issue with sleeping had picked up, but it couldn't be helped this time around. I was hoping that I would be able to sleep without too many problems.

The last thing I needed was the guys questioning if I could do my job or not. As far as they would know, I was completely stable and the picture of perfect health, and that was how I was going to keep it.

CHAPTER EIGHTEEN

Jarod

THE RED NUMBERS on the clock told me it was two in the morning. That clock was mocking me, I swear.

I should be exhausted.

I was tired, but I couldn't get my mind to turn off enough for me to fall asleep. I generally read when I got like this, but when you are sharing a hotel room with your new boss, you couldn't exactly leave the light on so you could read.

Not being able to read meant I couldn't get my mind to shut up.

I couldn't stop going over the case and what our next moves should be if this turned out to be a bust.

What if we couldn't find Vilenti?

Where would we go from there?

Or what if we did find Vilenti and he didn't talk, or he didn't know where Monroe was. I had all of these questions and I had no answers to any of them. I didn't know what the answers would be. I hadn't been able to truly learn while being a detective, because no one in the station wanted to actually teach me anything.

I knew I could have asked Mason or the guys, but I wasn't too comfortable with voicing my questions, just yet. I knew Mason said to ask questions and voice our opinions, but I was still waiting to be told to shut up. I was still waiting to get the same lecture that I had heard a hundred times since I had been promoted.

That I was useless and unimportant.

It wasn't something I could get over in a day or two. It was going to take time, which all seemed pointless because I was only on the task force for this one case. The task force was put together to find Monroe and once we did, there wouldn't be a point in the task force any longer. All of this stressing would be for nothing.

I let out a soft sigh as I rolled over onto my back once more. I was trying to be as quiet as possible so Mason wouldn't be kept awake as well. He had lain down with Koda around midnight and had been asleep ever since. I envied him for being able to fall asleep so fast.

I wished I could do that.

"Can't sleep, either?" Mason's husky voice broke the silence.

How was it possible this man could be even sexier in the middle of the night?

I rolled over so I was facing his bed and saw that he had done the same, without me noticing, as if he was some type of ninja. Hell, maybe he was before all of this. I didn't even know him. I knew his brother had been in the Army before he was a cop.

"I can't get my mind to stop racing," I admitted.

Mason gave a soft hum before he spoke.

"It's a common problem with smart people like yourself. Your mind is going all day long and that makes it hard to shut it off at the end of the day. There's not exactly an off switch you can flip."

My God, he got it.

He actually understood without me having to tell him what was going on with me.

I didn't think this man could get anymore perfect.

I really didn't.

I had lost count of how many times I had lost a boyfriend because of how I slept at night. They always made it seem like something was wrong with me because I could just lie down and cuddle with them. The ones who wanted to cuddle, anyway.

My romantic life had been a series of bad boyfriends and one-night stands that I picked up in a bar. I had not been lucky in love, but at the same time, I hadn't really been trying.

"Be great if there was," I commented back.

"Yeah, a magical switch that can be flipped, and for a good eight hours you stop thinking about anything. That'd be nice to have."

I couldn't help but wonder if Mason had his own issues with sleeping at night. The way he sounded, it made me feel like something more was going on with him. Like he was in desperate need of a switch to flip to get his mind to stop, too.

"I would have to imagine with the type of cases you get, you must see some pretty horrible things," I said with complete understanding lacing my voice.

I didn't know what it was like for him. What it was like to see children hurt and chase after criminals to try and save more innocent lives. I would have to imagine, though, that it took a toll on a person.

It couldn't be easy.

Nope, not at all.

"I am not a stranger to all-nighters or having a hard time getting to sleep. I try to relieve stress when I can, but it doesn't always work that way when you travel as much as I do."

"Your stress relief doesn't travel with you?" I asked, slightly confused by that.

"No, the TSA frowned upon me putting random guys into my suitcases," he lightly joked.

"Ah, that kind of stress relief. And here I was foolishly using a book. I should keep a good looking guy tied up in my room," I teased back.

I wasn't hiding being gay, and with

Mason gay as well, there was no point in denying it or tiptoeing around it. It wasn't like he was going to care. Besides, it was nice to be able to talk about being gay with someone.

I didn't really have any friends that I could be honest and open with. I didn't have a true partner on the force to share any personal details of my life with. It was just me and my mother, and she was not someone I was about to open up with.

"I find that is the best way to get a good night's sleep. You just gotta let him go when you are done so you don't have to worry about kidnapping charges."

"Is that what you do? Keep someone tied up in your bed and let them go when you have shown them all the pleasure in the world?"

I was willing to bet my life that Mason

was amazing in bed. He seemed like the type of guy that could throw you around and make your eyes roll into the back of your head. Sex with him was probably earth shattering, ruining you for other men.

"More often than not, it helps to shut my mind off long enough for me to fall asleep afterward."

"I usually read, but your way sounds much more fun," I said, flashing a small smile even though I knew he couldn't see it.

I would have loved to know what his hands felt like against my skin, but I knew that he wouldn't be interested in someone like me. I was willing to bet he preferred small guys. Most tops who looked like him liked to have smaller guys. They either didn't like to have a larger guy underneath them, or they assumed the guy was a top. Not that I was very big, but I wasn't a small spinner, either. It could make for a bit of an awkward meet up if the guy I'm hooking up with believes I like to top.

"We should try and get some sleep. Morning is going to come a lot faster than you think," Mason said after a moment.

I let out a short hum in agreement, but I knew the chances of me sleeping were pretty slim. Now, my mind couldn't stop thinking about Mason and what he would be like in bed. My body was reacting to my thoughts and I was grateful for us being in the dark.

The only light was from the small streetlights that were on the other side of the window. We were on the third floor, so the lights were still bright enough to reach us, but just enough for us to be able to see the outline of the room.

I was thankful for the darkness, it was the only thing keeping Mason from seeing my growing hard on. Now, this night was going to be even longer and I would be waking up sexually frustrated come morning.

It was a good twenty minutes of nothing but pure silence when Mason's growly voice broke it once again as he turned the small lamp on that was between us.

"Do you have a boyfriend?"

"No. You?"

I wasn't sure why he was asking me. I guess he couldn't sleep any better than I could.

"I don't. You know, we're both single, we both can't sleep, we could do something to relieve stress together," he said, and I could see the heat in his eyes.

I knew exactly what he was talking about and my dick was instantly rock hard. Every logical excuse as to why this was a bad idea went through my head. He was currently my boss and he had the power to ruin my career, mostly. I had every reason to say *no*. To play it off as if he was joking and act like it never happened come morning. That was the most reasonable and responsible thing to do in this situation. And yet, I wanted to throw caution to the wind and allow this man to pound into me.

I didn't do reckless things.

I made sure to be safe and cautious with every single guy I had laid down with. This would be reckless and could come back to bite me in the ass one day.

"I only bottom."

Mason gave me the sexiest smile I had ever seen as he pushed the covers off of himself and made his way over to me. He pulled the covers off of me and then his body was covering mine. The second his lips touched mine, my whole body was on fire. It wasn't just the kiss, but the weight of him against my body.

I loved being with larger men, muscular men, feeling their weight, their strength on my body, it always brought comfort to me. I opened my legs to allow Mason's hips to touch mine. The second our dicks touched we both moaned. We were both already half-hard and Mason ground his chub down onto mine.

I moaned into his mouth as sparks flew all down my spine.

Mason broke the kiss far too soon for

my liking, leaning up to just gaze down at me for a moment.

I could see the heat in his eyes and I knew this was going to be earth shattering.

His hands were instantly going to my clothes and I sat up and started to remove his. We were only wearing t-shirts and sweatpants, so it took no time at all to get naked.

I thought he was glorious with his clothes on, but it was nothing compared to the view of his naked form. He was ripped with muscles all over his body. Even his thighs looked like they could squeeze the life out of someone. Then there was his dick. Just the sight of it was making my mouth water. It was beautiful, big and thick, and it was going to feel amazing inside of me. I couldn't help but lick my lips at the glisten of pre-cum on his tip.

"See something you like?" he asked with a cocky smirk.

"Very much so," I answered honestly.

He threaded his hand through my hair and kept a grip on it as he spoke. "Go ahead and get a taste."

That was all the permission I needed.

I licked my lips, my mouth watering in anticipation of his taste. He guided my head to his dick and I was instantly licking at his tip, pressing my tongue into the slit before sucking on it. I couldn't help but hum my appreciation at the sweet taste of his precum.

I needed more.

I started to take him further into my mouth and I didn't stop until I got all the way down to his base. He was gloriously big and I had to relax my throat so I would be able to take him all the way in.

Mason let out a groan as he started to lightly rock his hips. I couldn't help but moan and whimper as he took control.

I loved it when a man was in charge. I was a bottom. I couldn't help it. I loved to be dominated and I loved when the man I was with took control. I had always been like that and I stopped trying to understand why a long time ago.

"You like that, eh? You like when I fuck your mouth," Mason panted out as he moved his hips faster.

A begging whine escaped my throat. I did like it when he fucked my mouth. He felt so good in my mouth and in my throat. I could do it all night long and never get tired of it. All too soon, though, he was pulling my head off of his cock and a small whimper escaped me at the loss of him in my mouth.

He sat back and grabbed his pants, pulling out a crumpled condom wrapper and a packet of lube. I watched as his shoulders suddenly slumped as he unfolded the condom.

"I'm sorry, Jarod, I don't have any condoms. This one is damaged and I didn't stop to pick up any, for logical reasons. I didn't expect to hook up while on a case. In fact, it's been a long time since I've been with anyone so grabbing condoms was kind of the last thought on my mind when I packed for this trip."

The man's sudden explosion of diarrhea of the mouth was truly sexy.

"Me either," I breathed out, and my breath hitched.

I wanted this.

I wanted Mason, and I wanted him now.

Could I forgo using a condom?

Did I trust this man enough to do that?

"I swear to you, I've always used them before, and I get tested regularly. I'm negative," he said.

"So am I."

"You sure you're okay with that?" He tilted my face up with a finger, cupping my cheek in his palm, and concern filled his eyes where before there was nothing but unbridled desire.

I knew I should be saying *no*.

I had never had sex without a condom on before. I always practiced safe sex, even though it'd been a really long time since I'd been with anyone. Still, there was this uncontrollable need within me to feel Mason's skin inside of me. I wanted to feel the heat of his cum buried deep inside of my ass.

Screw logic, tonight I was just going to feel.

"Yes," I simply said.

"On your knees, I want your ass up," he ordered, relief filling his features, and I was instantly following his command.

I felt him get off the bed as I got onto my hands and knees. I bent down on my elbows so my ass was up and on display to him. A moment later, I felt his hands grip my thighs and then he was yanking me to the edge of the bed. I felt his weight on the bed once again, followed by the sound of the lube packet being ripped open.

Mason placed his hand on my ass and ran it over my cheek before he gave it a light slap, causing me to whimper and involuntarily buck my hips.

"You like that, eh?" he asked in a husky, lust-filled voice.

"Yes," I said breathlessly.

He then slapped my ass even harder and I let out a deep moan.

I loved being spanked. I'm sure there was a Shrink somewhere just dying to get their hands on me.

He did it a few more times, each harder them the next, and it only resulted in my dick dripping with precum onto the bed.

"Such a pretty pink," he said as he ran his hands over the heat on my ass cheeks.

"Spread these cheeks for me," Mason demanded, sliding one digit down my crease.

I easily moved and grabbed my ass, spreading my cheeks so he had a clear view of my hole. A moment later, I felt the tip of his lube covered finger pushing inside of me. I sucked in a breath, reveling in the slight burn as he pushed his finger all the way inside of me.

Some bottoms preferred to only have a dick rather than a finger in them. To me, I didn't care what it was as long as it felt amazing.

Mason worked my ass quickly. I knew he was in need just as badly as I was. He quickly added a second finger and started to scissor me so I would be able to accommodate his large dick. When he added a third finger, he hit my sweet spot dead on and I saw stars as heat sizzled up my spine.

"Mason," I moaned.

"I'm going to pound the hell out of you," Mason promised.

"Fuck, yes, please," I begged.

There was nothing that I wanted more than to feel him inside of me. I needed to have sex, I needed to feel a very large dick inside of me and Mason definitely had that.

He removed his fingers from my ass and he then placed his hand on the back of my neck, possessing me and keeping me in this position. I couldn't contain the moan that escaped from my lips. It was like he just knew exactly what I needed.

I felt the crown of his shaft against my hole and it was only a second later when he was pushing inside of me. My eyes closed at the pleasure that surged through me.

He felt so good.

His rigid steel under velvet skin member pushing outward against the heat of my walls, the feeling of fullness, and the burn of the stretch, everything felt like Heaven and I never wanted to leave.

"You're so tight, Baby. It's been a while since you've had a big cock inside of you, eh?"

"Ooh, yes, way too long. Don't stop," I begged.

I needed to feel all of him.

"I'm not stopping until my cum is leaking out of this tight little hole," he promised and that only made me whimper with need.

Once he bottomed out, his balls pressed up tight against my taint, Mason kept his word.

He didn't go slow.

He pulled out almost all of the way before he slammed back in. His pace was fast and rough, and I loved every single second of it.

I couldn't contain the moans, even if my life depended on it. It felt too good. It felt amazing, beyond amazing, and I never wanted it to end. When his dick hit my glands dead on, I had just managed to turn my head into the bed as I screamed in pleasure.

"That's it, Baby, scream for me. Let everyone in this hotel hear how much you love my dick pounding into your ass," Mason said as he picked up his pace even more, snapping his hips and slamming into my ass.

He made sure each thrust hit my prostate and I couldn't stop screaming out. I had never felt this good, not even by my own hand. Mason was playing my body like an instrument and I loved it. I was craving more and he gave me more than I could ever ask for.

I could feel my legs shaking with my need to come. I wanted to touch myself, but I didn't dare. I wanted to see if Mason could do what no man had ever been able to do before. I wanted to know if Mason could make me come without touching my dick. If he could milk me simply from the pleasure he brought from fucking me.

I had lost track of time. The only thing in the world that existed was me and Mason in the hotel room. Time held zero meaning to me. All that I could feel was overwhelming pleasure and it all boiled over when Mason hit my sweet spot with even more force.

I gave a loud scream as I felt my dick

pulse and come. I couldn't stop moaning and writhing, bucking my hips and pushing backward as my dick was milked by Mason's thrusts.

He let out a deep moan as he continued hitting my sweet spot even faster.

"Fuck, that's it, Baby. Come for me."

Every time he knocked my sweet spot, it made me come even more. I couldn't believe how this felt. I'd suspected that Mason would be remarkable in bed, but I had no idea it would be this remarkable. It was earth shattering and he was going to ruin me for other men. From this point forward, I was never going to get this level of pleasure from any other man ever again in my life.

I was officially ruined.

Mason's thrusts were becoming more

erratic and I knew he was close. A few thrusts later, when he was snapping his hips forward and back in a rapid beat, I felt a wash of heat hitting my walls.

"Fuck," Mason growled as his dick throbbed inside of me.

Feeling his come inside of me made me feel owned.

Like I now belonged to him.

It should have bothered me, but it only made me even more turned on. I wanted to belong to him. I wanted only him to use my body, and no one else.

Mason spoke as he kissed along my spine.

"You feel so good, Baby. So tight and hot. A perfect little ass."

"You feel so good inside of me," I easily agreed.

"And we're just getting started."

"What?" I asked, even though I felt that he was still half-hard inside of me.

"I told you, you were going to have my cum dripping out of you. That doesn't happen after only one time. We got at least two more rounds to go."

"Oh fuck, yes," I whined.

I didn't want this to end. He could have tied me up and left me here for the rest of my life and I would have died happy. We needed sleep, yes, but fuck it, sleep was overrated. This was a night I was never going to forget and would happily submit to Mason for the rest of it.

CHAPTER NINETEEN

Mason

WORDS COULD NOT describe how last night felt.

I knew suggesting that we have sex so we could try and sleep would be a bad idea, but I had no idea it would be bad for this reason. I figured it would make things awkward between us or Jarod would get the wrong idea. I wasn't looking for a relationship. I never was.

But that didn't happen.

It wasn't awkward. In fact, it felt like a normal night for us. As if we always had sex and then go to work the next day. Which was odd, because I had never felt like that before with anyone. The bad part, though, I was already craving his body. As a rule, I could have sex with someone and then forget about it the next day, but for some reason my body was not looking to forget about Jarod's body underneath mine.

When he said he only bottomed, I expected what typically happened with guys his size. They like the bottom, but they still like to be in control. I didn't really enjoy sex with men who wanted to top from the bottom. With Jarod, though, he loved to bottom. He loved to be submissive, to let me control everything, and it was that fact that was driving me crazy for more.

I thought it would only be one time, one night, but I couldn't do that. I was going to need to have him again. There was no way I could not feel him underneath me again.

Soon.

For now, though, I had to focus on what was going on for today.

We had arrived in Columbus about four hours ago and, so far, all we had accomplished was my ass going numb from sitting in the car for so long. We were here to find Jose Vilenti. He had been in touch with Monroe quite frequently and I was hoping that meant he knew more about him than the others.

We needed to grab Vilenti so I could

get Monroe's information out of him. Vilenti wasn't a major criminal. He had his hands in a few different organizations. He was a labor man; someone that floated around and took work wherever it was needed. It worked in our favor because that meant he didn't hold any loyalty to one organization over another. He went where the money was and right now, there was not going to be any money from Monroe.

"Is this guy ever going to show?" Rafe commented over the coms.

I knew the others were getting restless.

I couldn't blame them.

Stakeouts were the worst, especially when said stake out was in a desert. It was hot and there was nothing to look at to try and keep you entertained. There were no people walking around, nothing.

It was just hot and made your body hurt from sitting for so long. Vilenti was set to show, though, so everyone was going to have to suck it up.

"He'll be here, relax," I said.

"Can I ask you something?" Jarod said from his seat next to me.

"I told you, you can ask any question you want."

"If Vilenti works for all of these different criminal organizations, how are you going to get him to roll on Monroe? Wouldn't he be even more worried about talking to the police with all of his connections?"

It was a logical question. Most people refuse to snitch when they are loyal to just one organization. Vilenti had multiple organizations that could try and kill him if word got out he was talking to the police.

"Technically, he has more to worry about with having multiple criminals that could come after him. However, because he floats and has all of these criminal connections, those organizations might not suspect him as being the snitch. He has a lot that could come after him, but he also has the protection that he's so low on the importance list that he can easily be overlooked as the snitch," I explained.

"He's protected by the numbers above him," Jarod said, nodding with complete understanding.

"Do you think he will talk?" he asked.

"I'll get it out of him," I said confidently.

"You sound so confident. I don't even think I would know what to say to someone in an interrogation."

"You've never done one before?"

It wasn't really that surprising. He worked in a small town.

I mean, seriously, what did they have to interrogate someone for?

Cow tipping?

If they did, in fact, buy a hooker?

There wasn't much at stake in a town like Gaithersburg.

"No, I've never seen one being done. I'm not really allowed to get that close to a case. I usually just handle paperwork."

"Because that is all they will allow you to do. I've seen your file and I know that you have helped other stations with cases. You have more closes under your belt than what that file says. You let people push you around, so they will naturally take advantage of that. It's why you have to stand up for yourself, Jarod. Be dominant at work and keep all of your submissiveness for the bedroom," I said that last part with a sexy smirk as heat filled his cheeks.

"I guess I've always been submissive in life. I don't like confrontation. Growing up, I did what I was told and stayed out of the way. I guess I'm just used to being ignored and doing what I'm told," Jarod reluctantly admitted.

I could see how it would be hard for someone like him. He didn't have much confidence in himself. He knew he was skilled, but even that lacked confidence. He was so much better than he gave himself credit for. Again, though, that could be connected to his intelligence.

"Not liking confrontation can be hard when you need to stand up for yourself. You're a genius, Jarod, that can make for a difficult time socially. You don't interact like the other guys at the station do, so you don't know how to connect with them. You just need to find your people and they will protect you from the assholes of the world."

"I don't want protection, though. I should be able to protect and defend myself," he said, and I could hear the self-hatred edging his tone.

"You have to learn how to stand up for yourself and part of that is feeling safe while doing it. That's where the protection comes in. If you knew without a doubt that whenever Baxter said something homophobic that you could punch him and nothing would happen to you, then you would do it. You would tell him to shut the hell up, because you knew that your people would keep you safe from him. The first step in standing up for yourself, is allowing that protection to come from people."

It wasn't easy to learn if you had never experienced it when you were younger. I could tell by the way Jarod interacted with the guys on the team that he didn't get many social interactions growing up. In high school, and even grade school, kids naturally flocked to their own kind. Jarod would have interacted with the other smart kids in the school. Unfortunately, that would have only added a bigger target on his back from jocks and bullies. And smart kids didn't have the social skills or the physical fitness to stand up for themselves and their friends. There wasn't really a set protector in the group and that resulted in adults who didn't know how to stand up for themselves.

I wasn't sure how long I would have with Jarod, but I was going to make sure he knew that I was there for him. Even if he didn't want to be on the task force after this, I was still going to be in his corner, protecting him. And when I couldn't be in town, I would make sure Roland was watching over him.

"It's a learning process, I guess. I always thought I wasn't too bad at interacting with different people. I'm good with victims, but the other cops at the station, I guess I just go back to my high school days where I kept my head down and did what I was told. The bullies didn't beat you up if you did their homework," he said with a small shrug.

"Here's what your fellow cops won't tell you. They aren't allowed to touch you, otherwise they would lose their job. The cops in your station, Jarod, they're all bark. They lost their teeth a long time ago. They have nothing to bite at you with. All you have to do to get them to shut up is hit them with a rolled up newspaper and show your teeth."

"A dog analogy from a K9 handler, I'm shocked," he lightly teased.

"Don't make me get the newspaper out," I warned playfully.

"I guess that would depend on where you're going to hit me with it," he said with a cocky grin.

I couldn't contain the groan that escaped my body. My mind was flooded by the sounds of his moans and whimpers from every time I slapped his ass last night. He did like to be spanked, and I loved spanking. It was like he was made for me and that should have scared me, but it didn't.

I had no idea what was happening. I had never felt like this before with anyone I had been with, not even my long-term fuck buddies. There was something special about Jarod and my body wanted an endless supply of him.

"We got movement at your ten o'clock, Boss," Ryzen's voice came over the coms.

I turned to look out of my window and I saw Vilenti walking over and sitting down on a picnic table. The area was deserted, so I knew we wouldn't have to worry about anyone getting the jump on us. He was there to wait for a shipment of drugs and when he wasn't there, the drug runners would wait for further instructions.

"Move in," I said over the coms.

We all got out of our vehicles and

made the distance toward Vilenti. I thought he would run when he saw us coming, but apparently the man was too lazy for it. Not that I minded. I wasn't in the mood to chase after him in this heat.

"Jose Vilenti," I started.

"Fed," he said with a nod.

"You're coming with us back to El Paso for questioning," I stated.

"Questioning for what? I haven't done anything. Unless it's illegal to pull over for some fresh air and a smoke?" he said with a smirk.

Technically, we couldn't arrest him. He wouldn't have anything on him that we could use for grounds for an arrest. He also had no outstanding warrants.

Vilenti had been careful in his criminal life. He only had a couple arrests as a juvenile and the records were sealed.

Nothing as an adult, and at thirty-eight, that was impressive. He was smart, but I suspected it was more than that.

"I didn't say you were under arrest, I said we're going to question you. I don't need to charge you with anything to do that."

"Get up," Rafe said as he grabbed Vilenti's bicep and lifted him off of the picnic table.

Vilenti was not a big guy and when you were Rafe's size, you could throw a grown ass man around like a rag doll. He slapped some cuffs on him before we all headed off for our vehicles.

We now had Vilenti and I would be getting any intel he had on Monroe out of him. I was not about to let that son of a bitch slip away. Vilenti would talk or I would make sure he didn't live very long once we let him go.

If he was as smart as he thought he was, he would spill and live to see another day.

CHAPTER TWENTY

Jarod

THE DRIVE BACK to the Homeland Security Field Office in El Paso was done in silence. It wasn't an awkward silence, though, so I was happy for it.

I wasn't sure what this morning would be like with Mason after last night. I wasn't sure if it would be awkward or uncomfortable. I hadn't been with someone in a good chunk of time so the whole 'morning after' scenario was pretty new to me.

I didn't expect for it to feel so comfortable, though. Routine, almost. As if that had always been our morning. It made no sense, because we barely knew each other, but I couldn't help but feel like we were kindred spirits, in a sense.

I wasn't expecting the connection, but I also wasn't expecting for him to be so understanding and insightful about who I was.

Most people didn't understand my mind. They didn't understand how my intelligence did make it hard for me during different social situations. I was so used to having to be quiet all the time. Having to take up as little space as possible so my parents wouldn't see me.

It had been the same in school.

Bullies were everywhere, so I stayed hidden. I stayed in the library when I could. I didn't go to social parties. I was the awkward smart kid who was an easy target for everyone in the school.

I thought when I became a cop that it would be different.

I figured that cops wouldn't be bullies. I thought that they would understand and accept that everyone was different and it would be okay. I thought that I would have finally found my place in the world.

My family.

But I had only been proven wrong.

It was like school all over again, and I had fallen into the same patterns that worked for me while I was in school. It never even crossed my mind that I should be standing up for myself. That I could stand up for myself without the fear of being hit.

It was a nice thought, but what Mason didn't know was that it wasn't true.

I had stood up for myself a few times with Baxter, but he had hit me. There had been a good handful of times that I'd had a black eye or a bruise on my cheek that I had to lie about.

I didn't know what I was going to do after the task force was completed. I knew the abuse with Baxter would get worse, because I would have had a hand in arresting his best friend. A man, despite all of the evidence, he still believed was innocent.

That was a problem for another day.

When we arrived, we all headed up to our area. I went with the others to the interrogation viewing room on the other side of a two-way mirror.

Mason took Vilenti into the interrogation room and attached the cuffs to a metal hoop in the center of the table. This was going to be my first interrogation and I was looking forward to seeing Mason's technique. This could very well be the only interrogation that I got to view if Monroe decided not to give himself up. I wanted to learn as much as possible.

"Jose Vilenti, I am Supervisory Special Agent Mason Wright with Homeland Security. You are here today because you have been in contact with a fugitive that we have been tracking, Jasper Monroe," Mason started.

"Never heard of him," Vilenti instantly said and I rolled my eyes. Of course he would say that.

"We have your phone number in his

burner phone. We already know that you have spoken with him on numerous occasions. Just like we know he has been using the foster children he had taken in to cook cocaine and sell it. He has also been selling children to a sex trafficking ring and has killed numerous other children who threatened to expose him. We can do this whole dance if you want, but do you really want to protect a child murderer? Do you really want to protect someone that is selling children to be raped and, eventually, killed?"

"Why would he care?" I couldn't help but ask.

Vilenti was a criminal. He was connected to a lot of criminal organizations that did all sorts of things.

So why would he care about Monroe's crimes?

"Believe it or not, but criminals also have a code. It's why in prisons they have to put child molesters and child abusers in solitary confinement to ensure they don't get killed. You could murder a thousand people and no one would care. But if you killed a child, if you molested one, they'll all try to kill you," Rafe started.

"Children are meant to be innocent and protected, even criminals know that. None of them will try and protect someone like Monroe. Mason isn't going to waste time trying to dance around. Sometimes, it's easier to tell someone the truth and let their moral compass do the work. It doesn't work for every crime, but in this situation it does," Cooper added.

That made sense, but I wasn't sure if it would work. We had no idea what Vilenti had done for Monroe. He could have been helping him hide children that were to be sold, for all we knew. Still, it was an interesting piece of knowledge that I would be keeping with me.

"Let's just say that I did know a Monroe, I didn't know he was into any of that," Vilenti started carefully.

"You are a small-time fish, Vilenti. I don't care what you do for the other organizations you work for. I don't care about the shipment of drugs you are supposed to be picking up, right now. I don't care that you were running drugs for Monroe. All I care about, is getting this son of a bitch and finding the kids that he sold like cattle. If you give me what I need, you can walk right out of here. You still got enough time to get back to Columbus and make it look like you were fashionably late," Mason said.

I could see Vilenti was thinking about it, but I knew he would take it. You could tell he wanted to get out of here, and if he had to roll on Monroe, then he would do it. I was hoping he would be able to tell us something that we could use to find Monroe. I didn't want to go on a scavenger hunt for this man.

"I knew about him making drugs, but I didn't know he was a foster parent or any of that stuff with the kids. If I had known, I would have killed him. I was just picking up the drugs and running the money to where it needed to go. I don't know where he is, but I know he's connected to some big hitters."

"How do you know that?"

"Because when I would run the money, it was always fifty grand and it was given to the same guy. He's a runner for the Sinaloa Cartel down in Mexico. He's the border guy. There's always talk within the grapevine about who the new members are of the cartels. Monroe, though, he's an old guy with them. Everyone who is anyone knew of him. He had been around for decades and all of the runners knew better than to cross him. As far as we all knew, he was a drug leader for the cartel for the East Coast."

If he was connected to a cartel, this was going to be even more complicated. I didn't know much about cartels, but I knew that their reach went very far. They had cartel members all over the country and there was no telling where Monroe could be hiding out.

"Where is he?" Mason asked.

"I don't know. He sent me a text,

though, letting me know his new number. I can give you the number."

Mason pushed the pad of paper and a pen over to Vilenti as he spoke.

"If you hear from him before we grab him, you're going to text me. I need him alive so I can try and track down the children he sold."

"I got ya," Vilenti agreed.

Mason handed him his card before he got up. He removed the cuffs and walked him out of the room.

We all headed out of the viewing room and Mason handed Cooper the pad of paper before he walked off with Vilenti to let him go. The rest of us moved to the conference room and Cooper was instantly going to his laptop to try and find Monroe from his new number.

"Could Monroe really be connected to a

cartel?" Hollingsworth asked.

"People who make drugs are generally connected to a gang or a cartel. They have the market and it's not like you can open a mom and pop drug making business," Rafe answered.

"How would he have even gotten involved with a cartel, though? He's always lived in Gaithersburg," Hollingsworth asked next.

"You'd be surprised what people can do in their free time. He could have had a friend from growing up that is in a cartel now. You never know where your childhood friends will end up," Rafe answered again.

True, but this seemed really farfetched. He had to have gotten involved with them, somehow. He had to cross paths with someone that got him involved and he must have gone from the ground up. We had no idea how high he went, but if Vilenti was tight, he was supplying drugs to the East Coast. That was no small feat and he had a lot more runners than just the kids he was fostering.

Mason walked into the room roughly five minutes later and I could tell he was itching to move. We were getting closer with each lead we found and this could be what brought us to Monroe finally.

"You got him, Coop?" he asked.

"The phone is on. He's not expecting for us to ever find the new number. I'm tracking it, now."

"Do you think he'll be local?" I asked Mason.

"I doubt it. If he's connected to the Sinaloa Cartel, he could be anywhere," Mason answered.

"Aw, shit," Cooper said from his spot.

"How bad?" Mason asked.

I had no idea how he knew that whatever Cooper found was going to be bad, but apparently, they had already developed a shorthand with each other.

"I can't pinpoint a physical address. That will take a lot more work to get, but I know what town he's in," Cooper started.

"Where?" Mason asked.

"Mexico City."

"As in Mexico?" I asked, shocked.

If Monroe wasn't in the States, did that mean we couldn't go after him?

I had no idea what type of reach the task force had, but I knew as a cop, I could only operate within the United States.

"The one and only. It's going to take me time to find a physical address, Boss,"

Cooper answered.

"That's fine. Everyone pack up and let's get to the airport. We need to get to Mexico City. When we get there, Coop, start looking for Monroe by his phone. The rest of us will see who he could be connected to in Mexico City. We know he's most likely connected to the Sinaloa Cartel, so let's see what stash houses they have where they could be hiding him," Mason said.

Apparently, we could operate in Mexico.

Holy shit, I was going to Mexico.

I had never been outside of the country and I didn't think a manhunt would be my reasoning for it. This task force was bringing me a lot of firsts and I had no idea how I was ever going to survive going back to being just a detective in

Gaithersburg.

I was going to die of boredom after all of this.

We all started to pack up the conference room before we would need to do the same for our hotel rooms. We were going to Mexico and, hopefully, we would be able to bring Monroe to justice.

CHAPTER TWENTY-ONE

Mason

"HOW WAS THE flight?" Roland asked.

We had landed roughly two hours ago and had settled into the hotel for the night. Tomorrow, we would be trying to locate Monroe in Mexico City. I was hoping he was laying low somewhere and not in a Sinaloa Cartel stronghold. That would make everything more complicated and I wasn't certain we would be able to extract him without getting everyone killed. I would have to wait and see where Monroe was hiding out. Maybe we would get lucky and he was sitting in some motel, somewhere.

When we had gotten in the room, I had set up my laptop and video called Roland to see what he had.

"It was fine. Any news?"

I was hoping to get some good news from him. It was sad that good news in this case would be to locate a mass grave of children's remains, but it would at least be something. Depending on how Monroe killed them, there might be evidence still left on their bodies. Evidence we could use to put the final nail into his coffin. It was one thing to try and play dumb about drugs being made in your own basement, it was another to have evidence of you killing a child. He wouldn't be able to talk his way out of that. And no jury in the world would believe he didn't kill and bury all of the kids, if we had evidence that connected him to one single body.

"Damien and Sebastian were able to locate the mass grave for the children. It was approximately forty-five minutes from town, in a clearing in the woods. They went in with ground penetrating sonar to locate the grave. They haven't started to dig yet, though. They wanted to see what you wanted them to do. But Mase, Damien said it looks like there's close to a hundred remains in the clearing."

"A hundred?" Jarod said as he got up off the bed and joined me at the table.

That was a lot higher than I was expecting. I knew Tyler had said that

Monroe had killed a few when they became too much of a risk, but I didn't know it would be anywhere near that number. He had clearly been killing kids a lot longer than we expected.

"Is Damien sure they are children and it's not a Native burial ground?" I asked.

I wasn't sure if the woods that Damien located the bodies in were sacred at some point in history. It wouldn't be the first time I had been looking for a mass grave and stumbled upon a native burial ground.

"Damien isn't an expert at reading skeletons from sonar, but he did say they were small. None of them appeared to be large enough for an adult. There's also no markings in the area to indicate that it is sacred ground. Sebastian also did some research, but nothing has come up that would lead us to believe that Natives are buried there."

"But a hundred? How could he kill that many kids and no one noticed anything? Gaithersburg isn't exactly a big town, someone had to have noticed the children missing at some point," Jarod commented.

He took the words right out of my mouth.

I knew Monroe had been a foster parent for close to twenty years, but a hundred kids, that was five kids a year. Five kids every year that went missing, all before they were old enough to be a legal adult. It wasn't like Monroe was taking on seventeen year olds that you could kill and say they aged out. He was taking kids under fourteen. You can't kill kids that young and have it go unnoticed. Someone should have noticed that Monroe was losing five kids every year. There was clearly a pattern. No one was that unlucky that they had that many kids go missing every year.

"There's no way he doesn't have someone on the inside in Social Services," I said.

"I ran every name with Social Services, starting with Tyler's social worker at the time. Everyone came back clean. However, Isaiah and I have been going over every file for every child that Monroe took in. It's close to three hundred kids. All have come from towns all around us, all with different social workers. However, the ones that Tyler remembered being killed or sold, they all had the same Social Worker. That Social Worker died of cancer three months ago."

"So what, Monroe made sure to only kill those kids?" Jarod asked, confused.

"Did he cover the other kids up?" I asked, because that was weird to me, as well. Monroe wouldn't have been able to predict which kids would be at risk of talking. Yes, he could pick which kids he was going to sell, but you couldn't control what kid would open their mouth or not.

"We're just starting to really trace everything. It's a big ass paper trail, but from what we can tell, some of the kids that have gone missing were transferred over to that Social Worker. A David Burn. He had been working for Social Services for thirty years. I suspect that Monroe and Burn knew each other and were in on it all together. I'm working on getting Burn's finances and going through them to see if he got any money outside of his paycheck."

"All right, chase it down. We need to know if anyone else within Social Services has been helping Monroe. I don't want to leave any dirty Social Workers behind. We need to do a clean sweep of all Social Services in the surrounding towns, too. I'll let my boss, Keyes, know what is going on and he'll help you if anyone wants to give you trouble handing the files over."

I wasn't about to allow anyone to hurt or exploit a child. If there were more dirty Social Workers, I was going to find them and make sure they paid for their crimes. They were supposed to be there for children in need. They were not supposed to add more pain to their lives.

"I'll handle it. What do you want us to do about the grave? Do you have someone that could handle the recovery, because we sure as hell don't."

"I'll put the call in and have a forensic team and an anthropologist down there to handle the recovery and look over the bodies. Collect all of the files for the children that have disappeared and see about any dental records for them. The anthropologist will need something to identify the bodies with."

"I'll get right on it and try to have what they need by the time they arrive. Most haven't been reported missing. It looks like Burn just has them relocated to a place that doesn't exist. It's going to take time to figure out just how many have been sold over the past thirty years and if Monroe was the only foster parent doing this. We're going to have to go through all past and present foster parents to make sure none of them are dirty, as well."

That was going to be the issue.

It was a huge undertaking, but it was one we needed to take on. It wouldn't be instant, it was going to be a lot of long hours over months to go over every single file, but it had to be done. I couldn't control what happened outside of Gaithersburg's area, but I was going to be living there, now. That town was going to be my home and I was not about to let any child in my area be in danger.

Not while I could prevent it.

"We'll get everyone we can on it. Damien and Sebastian also have their own guys that can jump in to help go through the files. Isaiah had brought on Travis to help as well. We'll get it done, no matter how long it takes. Every child will be identified and buried properly," Roland said with determination in his voice.

"You're damn right we will. Get everyone you can on it. I'll get the team down there right away. They should arrive tomorrow morning just before noon."

"Everything else going okay where you are?"

"We're gonna track Monroe down tomorrow and, hopefully, we can easily extract him. I'll let you know when we have him. Keep an eye on Tyler. The closer we get, the more heat Monroe will feel."

"I have him in my eyesight at all times. Don't worry about us. you focus on grabbing Monroe. I love you, little brother."

"Love you, too."

"Keep an eye on him, Lopez," Roland said with a nod to Jarod next to me.

"I promise, Sir," Jarod easily said.

If Roland only knew just how much of an eye Jarod had been keeping on me. We said a quick goodbye before I ended the call.

Jarod went back to work on his own research while I made the call to Keyes and got him fully updated. He was going to get us a forensic team down to the mass grave and get us the best anthropologist to help make the identifications.

It was going to take time.

I knew some of the remains we wouldn't have any dental records for. Children who grew up in the foster system didn't often visit a dentist unless the foster parent had no choice. Some of the older remains were going to take a lot more work to try and identify, and the reality was, we might never be able to.

That was okay, though, because we would give them names and a proper burial.

We would make sure they were never forgotten again.

It was nearing eleven at night when my eyes could no longer focus to read. It had been a long few weeks and I hadn't been sleeping very well. That was the problem with being dyslexic. If I didn't get enough sleep, after a while the words all blurred together and the letters got mixed up. Reading became impossible.

I let out a sigh and rubbed my eyes to try and get them to wake back up.

"You okay?" Jarod asked from his spot on his bed.

"Yeah, I've just lost the ability to read," I said with a sigh.

"Can you read this to me?" I asked, pointing to an email that I was trying to read.

"Um... yeah, sure," Jarod said and I could tell he wasn't certain if I was playing around or not. He came and sat down next to me and I turned my laptop around so he could see it.

"All right, it says that Monroe has not been placed on any watch list. The feds in Mexico had no idea he could be connected to the Sinaloa Cartel. There's no file on him on any federal level."

"I didn't think there would be, but it had to be checked."

I could see the question in his eyes, but he wasn't going to ask. It wasn't something that bothered me nor was it something I had been trying to hide.

"I have dyslexia. When I get too tired, the words and letters get mixed up and I can't read."

"It's impressive that you've been able to become a federal agent with it. I know some learning disabilities can be really hard to overcome. Just goes to show how determined and resilient you are," he said with a warm smile.

This man was remarkable.

I was never sure how someone was going to react to hearing that I had a learning disability. There had been a point in my life where I couldn't read at all. Roland had been the one to spend hours with me, helping me learn how to rewire my brain so I could read. Most tended to think something was wrong with me, that I had been given special treatment for me to be a Fed. I didn't have a propensity to tell people about being dyslexic, but I suspected that Jarod wouldn't hold it against me.

"I think it's time to call it a night," I said as I closed my laptop.

"But how will we ever fall asleep?" Jarod said with a playful grin.

Having sex with him more than once could very well be dangerous. I knew that. But fuck, it was so good, and I had never slept better in my life.

We were only having fun.

There was no harm in that, right?

I couldn't help but smirk at him as I reached for my handcuffs that were sitting on the table.

"I can think of something," I said as I dangled the handcuffs off my index finger.

Jarod gave a soft whimper at the idea and I knew he was on board.

I stood as I spoke again.

"Strip."

"Yes, Sir," Jarod easily said with a

playful smirk.

Hearing the *Sir* coming out of his mouth only made my dick throb and grow hard.

He got up and started to strip for me, keeping his gaze on me as he removed each article of clothing. Once he was naked, I allowed myself to take in how beautiful his body was. How smooth his olive skin was.

I could still vividly remember how amazing his body felt against my own skin last night. How tight his ass was around my dick.

I could never get tired of it.

A dangerous thought, in and of itself, but I pushed that away, for now. The only thing that mattered was the naked body in front of me.

I removed my own clothes before I

grabbed some lube and then made my way over to Jarod. I placed my hand on the center of his chest and pushed him back toward the bed.

Tonight, we were going to do things a bit differently.

Once I got him down onto the bed by the headboard, I grabbed each of his wrists and brought them up to the post. I cuffed him so he wouldn't be able to remove his arms from the position I wanted him in. I then went and placed myself before his legs, legs that he eagerly opened for me.

I could see that he was already hard without me even having to touch him. He liked to be dominated and that only made him even sexier. I bent down so my mouth was just above his.

"Don't move," I demanded.

"Yes, Sir," he said in a breathy voice.

"Good boy."

I closed the small gap between us, pressing my lips against Jarod's. He was instantly hungrily kissing me back. I could feel the need in him was growing fast. He had clearly been sexually starving for a long time, now. Maybe he didn't get out much and had one-night stands, or the men he had been with couldn't give him the dominance his body was craving.

I couldn't blame him.

There had been too many times where I had to settle for something less than what I wanted in the bedroom. Sometimes, the need to have sex was too great to wait around for the right person to come along.

I pulled back and grabbed the lube. I slicked up three of my fingers and watched him as I inserted my index finger.

Jarod gave a throaty moan as I entered him and he wiggled his hips slightly.

"I said don't move," I said with a sharp edge to my voice.

"Sorry, Sir," Jarod easily said, and I could tell he was struggling not to push down and get my finger in further.

He was in a deep need tonight and that only fueled me on. If we hadn't been on a clock, I would have dragged this out for hours. I would have slowly finger fucked him until he was begging me to pound the fuck out of him.

However, sadly, we were on a clock.

We couldn't be awake all night having mind-blowing sex, so I would have to settle for a preview of what was to come.

I quickly added a second finger and

Jarod moaned and fought not to move his hips. He was able to keep himself still, though, and I rewarded him by adding my third finger.

"Oh god," he moaned as his pleasure was spiked. And again he stayed still like he had been told.

"That's my good boy. Tell me, what do you want?" I asked in a husky voice as my fingers just missed his sweet spot.

"You. I want you, Sir," he said with a whimper as I continued to move my fingers close to his sweet spot, but purposely never hitting it.

"To do what?"

"Fuck me, Sir."

"You mean like this?" I asked as I playfully circled around his prostate, just skimming it with my fingers.

"Oh, please. I need to feel your dick

inside of me, Sir."

The sweet begging coming off his lips was what did me in. I couldn't hold out any longer. I had to feel him, again. Next time, though, next time I was going to be dragging this out.

Once the case was closed, he was going to be all mine for a whole night.

I removed my fingers from his ass and grabbed the back of his thighs, lifting them up to his chest. The position put his ass completely on display and it also almost folded him in half. He was completely at my mercy, and I loved it.

What made it better was I knew he loved it, too.

I easily lined myself up with his hole and slowly pushed my tip in between the tight muscles. We both moaned at the glorious sensation and I knew there would be no holding back tonight.

"It's gonna be hard and fast. You feel too good," I warned.

"Fuck, yes. Fuck me, Sir."

I pistoned my hips forward, slamming every inch of my dick inside of him, relishing in the friction, and hitting his glands dead on.

Jarod gave a loud moan as he was finally getting exactly what he wanted.

He was so tight and hot.

I would never get tired of this.

I kept my pace fast and brutal. I knew this round was going to be quick, but I had no intention of going just one round. I wouldn't keep us up all night, but I was going to enjoy Jarod's body for a couple of hours.

I made sure to aim for his sweet spot each time, bringing him closer and closer to the edge.

"Oh fuck." Jarod moaned deeply as his cock pulsed and released some precum.

I knew he was close, his shaft was straining against its skin, the tip already purple and filled with blood, but he needed some help to get over the edge.

I snaked my hand around his hardness and started to jerk him off in unison with my thrusts.

"Come for me, my little Slut."

A shiver of pleasure shot throughout Jarod's whole body as he moaned at my words.

"Someone likes to be called a slut. Or maybe it's because you're *my* slut," I whispered against his skin as I pressed kisses along Jarod's neck.

"Yes, Sir, only yours," he said breathlessly as his legs trembled with the need to come.

He was so beautiful like this.

I had no idea he would ever be this much of a submissive bottom. He didn't look it, but he did like to be dominated, and his love of it was only driving me crazier.

"You're so close. Come for me, now."

Jarod gave a deep moan and a whimper as my words pushed him over the edge. Due to our position, though, his cum hit his face. Between the sight of his own cum on his face and the tightness of his walls around my dick, I was falling off the cliff right behind him.

I felt Jarod pulse out more cum as I came hard inside of him.

I was never going to get tired of this sensation. Of feeling how tight and hot he was. His walls hugged my dick like they never wanted to be without it.

We were both breathing heavily, but that never stopped me from continuing before.

"You look so sexy like this. Restrained with your own cum on your face. Most beautiful thing I have ever seen," I said as I bent forward and ran my tongue along his cheek to get some of his cum. I couldn't help but moan at the sweet taste of him. I hadn't tasted him before. Our first time, I wasn't certain how adventurous he was and it was more about just trying to burn off energy so we could sleep. But now, I knew he liked to be dominated. He liked being submissive, and that opened up a whole world of possibilities.

I moved and kissed him roughly and he melted into it. He eagerly opened his mouth when my tongue licked and chewed at his lips. The second my tongue was in his mouth, he let out a breathy moan as the taste of himself hit his tongue.

His tongue was licking at my own, trying to get every trace of taste off of it. At just the knowledge that he liked his own taste, I was rock hard again and ready for the next round.

Tonight was only a preview of what was to come for us, because once this case was closed, I was going to need at least a couple of days alone with him before I would be satisfied.

CHAPTER TWENTY-TWO

Jarod

THE SOUND OF groaning brought me out of a deep sleep.

I squinted my eyes open and saw that it was only three in the morning. I let out my own groan as I realized that I had only been asleep for an hour.

Mason and I had thoroughly enjoyed the other's body for close to two hours before we decided to call it a night. I knew what we were doing was stupid. I shouldn't be having sex with my boss, even a temporary boss, but Mason was too good to resist. His skills in the bedroom were off the wall amazing.

I was never going to regret it.

The groaning sound turned into moans of what sounded like pain.

I pushed myself up and looked over at Mason's bed. We didn't sleep next to each other, that wasn't what we were doing. What we shared was just sex, cuddling was off the table.

I could see Mason's brow creased, even in the darkness of the room. He was having a nightmare. I reached over and turned on the bedside light between us before I got up. I knew better than to shake a highly trained man while he was sleeping. Mason hadn't been in the military, but he was just as deadly. Koda's head had popped up and I figured maybe he would be able to help me.

"Koda, wake Mason up."

I knew Koda didn't have to listen to me, but thankfully, he jumped up from his spot on the bed and instantly went over to Mason. The German Shepherd laid down on Mason's chest, and started to nudge and lick at his face.

"Mason, come on, wake up," I said a bit loudly to try and help Koda get him awake.

It was a moment later when Mason's eyes snapped open and he shot up into a sitting position. He was breathing heavily and I could see his body trembling. Whatever the nightmare was, it was bad enough to affect his whole body.

"It's okay. You're in Mexico City," I said.

Mason looked over at me and I could see the confusion in his eyes starting to dissipate.

However, it did nothing for the deep pain that I saw there.

I needed to take that pain away.

I wanted to make it better.

I wanted to get rid of that pain from him.

There was this undeniable pull I had toward Mason. I had no idea what was going on between us. The connection I felt for him was so intense and it made no sense. We barely knew each other and yet, everything in me was screaming for him. I felt like I had known him my whole life, which was insane and not something that had ever happened to me before.

Mason looked around the room before his gaze landed on me. I could tell he was embarrassed about waking me up from him having a nightmare, but he had no reason to be. We all get them and I would be willing to bet my life that his nightmares were a direct result from the work that he did.

"Sorry," he said with a shaky voice.

"You have nothing to be sorry for. If I had to see half of the horrors that you have with doing this job, I would be terrified to close my eyes. You're really brave to keep doing this job."

"No, I'm not. I'm weak." Mason looked down as he spoke.

I moved so I was sitting on the bed in front of him before I spoke in a gentle voice.

"No, you're not. Why would you think

that?"

I could see the self-hatred flash through his eyes. Something more was going on with him. I couldn't help but be worried that something was wrong with him, that he had been hiding some type of medical condition. Because there was nothing he could tell me that would have me believing that he was weak. He was the bravest man I had ever met and there was nothing he could say that would ever change that.

"I was supposed to be on vacation when this case started. Everyone thinks I'm just taking some time to unwind, but an outside shrink diagnosed me with PTSD."

I could hear the self-hatred and disgust in his voice. He thought that made him weak. He thought it made him less of a man because he was experiencing problems from the horrors he had seen.

It wasn't even just what he had seen. I saw him naked. I had seen the scars. He had been in fights. He had experienced trauma along with the mental abuse he had experienced every day he went to work. The fact that he had been diagnosed with PTSD and he was still here, still fighting to find Monroe and save children, it only showed me how strong and dedicated he was to helping people.

I reached out and placed my hand on the side of his face as I spoke.

"That doesn't make you weak. The fact that you are here, still doing this job with PTSD, that makes you strong. Babe, the very last thing you are is weak."

"I don't want anyone knowing."

"Your secret is safe with me," I easily promised.

He gave me a small smile and I could tell he needed a distraction. He had just told me something very personal and it was only fair that I did the same for him. I didn't want to tell anyone this, but it only seemed fair to share something this personal with him after what Mason had just shared with me. I was also hoping that he wouldn't judge me or hold it against me. That he would understand what my father did was completely out of my control and it didn't mean that I would be a killer as well.

"My father was the River Walk Killer."

"What?" he asked, confused. I could tell he wasn't confused by the sudden change in topics, but what I had changed it to.

MASON

"Deigo Santiago. That was my father. I was fifteen when my mother and I discovered he was murdering people. Agent Morgan Torres from the FBI showed up on our doorstep with his arrest warrant. We thought they were confused, but then, in a secret hidden room in our basement, they found photos and a lock of hair from each of his victims. Ninety-three women were killed by his hands."

"Holy shit. I heard about that case. It was discussed in my training classes in the academy. It was huge. You changed your last name."

"I did, but not to my mother's maiden name. Lopez is actually my middle name. I didn't want anyone to be able to look up my name and find out who my father was. I've kept it quiet. I didn't want anyone to judge me for his actions. It's why I can't be in a federal agency or major city for work. There's too many chances that someone could figure it out."

"What happened after he was arrested?"

"A shitshow. My mother kept hoping that it was all some big misunderstanding. As if the photos and locks of hair were placed in a secret room in our home by a complete stranger. After my father was convicted to multiple life sentences, she started to spiral. They were never loving parents. They didn't want to be parents, but they had me. It was as if I was a cat that they had to adopt and just live with. I took care of myself and I made sure the bills were paid. I managed the money when my mother couldn't. She started to use heroin and when the mortgage got to be too much, she sold the house and moved into an apartment before I went to the police academy. When she used all of her money, she moved into an apartment that was disgusting and barely standing. She does heroin all day long and prostitutes to cover her usage and rent."

I hated that my own mother was a prostituting heroin addict. I hated that she paid her rent with her body and that she used so much heroin that she couldn't even keep up with the cash to pay for the drugs. That she would be beat up and have her life on the line, all for some brown powder. It never made sense to me and it never would.

"I'm sorry you had to go through that. She doesn't want to get clean?"

"No. I've tried. Three times I've put her through rehab, but she always relapses within thirty days. A few years ago, she was in the hole ten grand with her dealers. She was almost beaten to death, so I paid 'em off. She just kept using after that. She doesn't want to be sober. And I can't make her be sober. Eventually, the drugs will kill her or a John will, but there's nothing I can do about that. I have to focus on the people that I can save, the ones that want to be saved."

"Unfortunately, that's all you can do. She has to want to be sober, otherwise it won't work. But you already know that. I'm sorry you've had to go through that. But I want you to know that it doesn't change what I think of you. I'm never going to judge you based on your parents' actions. It's your own actions that dictate your character and you have shown me that you are a good man who wants to make the world a better place," Mason said with a warm smile and it instantly hit me right in my own heart.

This man couldn't get any more perfect.

It was too bad he was only interested in sex, because I would have definitely been interested in more. From the very little I knew about him, I wanted to know more. I wanted to know everything about him, the good and the bad.

"You're a good man, too, Mason. Your PTSD doesn't make you weak and it doesn't change that you are still putting yourself through the trauma of this job to help people. To save more children. You're a good man and I am lucky to have met you," I said, flashing him a warm smile.

He gave me one in return and I could see that bit of darkness and pain in his eyes starting to dissipate. It made me feel good to know that I had been able to help him through this bout of darkness, but I also knew it was only a drop in the bucket for him. He had a long road to go if he ever wanted to be fully recovered, but I was hoping I would be around to see some of it. That after Monroe was caught whatever was going on between us wouldn't be over. Even if it was just sex whenever he could be in town, it was better than nothing.

"We need sleep. We have a long couple of days ahead of us," he said after a moment.

I gave a nod. He was right, we had to get some sleep with what we had ahead of us. If Monroe was located in a dangerous area of the city, we couldn't risk being too tired or rundown. I went to get up, but

Mason's hand on mine stopped me.

"Sleep with me?" he asked, and I could hear the uncertainty in his voice. I hated hearing the vulnerability. It didn't belong on a man that had faced hell itself and survived.

"Absolutely," I said back.

He moved over and I got under the covers with him. I curled up against his chest and Koda lay down on the other side of him. I couldn't ignore how good it felt to have his arms around me. To hear his heartbeat thrumming under my ear as it soothed me to sleep. I never wanted to forget about this moment and I hoped, prayed, that it would happen again.

CHAPTER TWENTY-THREE

Mason

EVERYONE ON THE team was currently in my hotel room.

I didn't want to risk going into any field office where this cartel was concerned. I didn't want to risk being in any office where someone could be on the payroll. This cartel had a great deal of connections in order for them to evade arrests and be able to move their products over the border.

I wasn't taking any chances.

I didn't care about the cartel.

I cared about Monroe.

There was no point in trying to shut down the cartel. Whenever you take out one of the major players, someone else takes their place. It was an endless game of whack-a-mole and I had no interest in playing it. Unlike other criminal organizations that just run drugs or guns, the cartel wouldn't care that we only wanted Monroe.

I had reached out in previous cases to major drug runners and even weapon traffickers to try and find someone that was selling children. They all were helpful, especially when I told them I wasn't looking for them, nor cared what they were doing. They all provided me with information on my suspect because they hated anyone who hurt children. Cartels were different, though. Money was money to them.

"Any luck on the mass grave?" Rafe asked as he sat back with his coffee.

"Damien and Sebastian were able to locate a mass grave within an hour of town. I have a forensic team going down to handle it. It looks like a hundred bodies," I answered.

"A hundred? How the hell did he kill that many and it didn't get noticed?" Hollingsworth instantly asked.

"Roland is looking into it. But there was a Social Worker in a nearby town, Burn, that was helping Monroe with covering it up and giving him the kids that no one would miss. Roland is going to have to run a full investigation into the foster systems in town and in the surrounding ones. It's going to be a lot of work, but each foster parent and Social Worker will have to be investigated and cleared."

"That is a massive undertaking. It's going to take months before that can be completed," Rafe commented.

"I know. Roland is going to pull in everyone he can. Damien and Sebastian are going to help, as well. It's a process, but it has to happen. There's a bigger operation going on than just Monroe and it all needs to be stopped before more children are hurt or sold."

"It has to be done. We can help once we get back to the station," Jarod said as he indicated between him and Hollingsworth, who gave a nod in agreement.

"Shit," Cooper said from his spot behind his computer.

"Do I want to know?" I couldn't help but ask.

Cooper didn't say much when he was busy trying to track someone or something down, but when he did, it was either worth it or something I wasn't going to be happy about.

"I found Monroe," Cooper started.

"Great. Where is he?" Rafe asked, not sure what the big deal was.

"He's in a Sinaloa's stronghold where the head of the cartel lives, with about a hundred armed guards."

"Shit," Ryzen agreed.

"Are you sure he's there and it's not just his cell phone?" I asked.

"I found his cell phone there so I used

satellite images to confirm his presence. He is there, hiding out like a little bitch in a whore house," Cooper confirmed.

"What is he doing there, though? I know he's got a connection to the cartel, but why would they risk everything to hide him. They have to know he's wanted by now," Jarod asked.

That was what didn't make sense to me. Even Vilenti had said that Monroe was small-time. That he provided some drugs to him when his supplier was running low or it was easier to get them from Monroe than transporting drugs across the country. Cartel would use him to help fund their pockets, but if he was small-time, he wouldn't be worth having him in the stronghold. Cartel leaders keep their family in strongholds and their highest-ranking men.

Monroe shouldn't be there.

Not with the intel that we had.

"He's right. Cartel leaders don't let just anyone into their stronghold, especially outsiders," Rafe said.

"Unless he's not small-time. Maybe Monroe has been downplaying his connection to the cartel, or his role in it. We don't know how many kids have been sold over the past thirty years. We don't know if other Social Workers had a hand in it. Maybe Monroe has been supplying the cartel with kids," I said.

"Okay, but why? Why American kids?" Hollingsworth asked.

"They make more money," Ryzen answered.

"That's exactly it. Clients will pay far more for a white American child, especially ones with blond hair and blue eyes. And this cartel has ties to Brazil and Colombia, they could be sending the children all over the world to be traded and sold. The cartel can also use them to help manufacture and package the drugs. It's cheap labor and a huge profit for them. If Monroe is their connection to children that can go missing and no one reports, he's their connection to billions of dollars," I explained.

"But that connection is burnt now, though. It's not like Monroe can wait it out and go start over in another city. Not to mention, he's almost sixty, now. He won't be able to foster any more children soon. What worth is he to the cartel?" Hollingsworth asked.

"He's gotta be worth something for them to want him alive. As a rule, when someone has lost their worth to a cartel they kill 'em to ensure they don't talk. They don't hide him away," Cooper commented.

"Unless he is still worth something," Rafe stated.

"But what?" Jarod asked.

"What if Monroe isn't a player, but the head?" I said as my mind tried to work it out.

"Head of what?" Jarod asked, confused.

"Supply chain," Ryzen stated, but failed to explain. He really was a man of few words.

"Monroe had connections from being a cop for thirty years. He also had connections from being a foster parent and working within the drug trade. Foster parents and law enforcement go to conventions all over the country. Monroe could have been going to them and connecting with less than desirable foster parents to bring into the organization. He could be running a child trafficking ring and supplying the cartel with them. That would explain why the cartel is protecting him. He has all of those connections and without him communicating with those connections, the supply chain falls apart. Monroe doesn't have to take on any more children to still make money for the cartel. He just needs to be alive and not in jail," I explained.

"So he's a major player and the cartel wants to protect their future profits," Jarod stated, now fully understanding what was going on.

"He's going to be a real bitch to get out," Hollingsworth stated what we were all thinking.

"We gotta get him out, anyway. Coop, I want satellite images of the area and a schematic to the stronghold. We go in tonight to grab him," I stated.

"Alone?" Hollingsworth asked, shocked.

"We can't go in alone. There's too many of 'em," Rafe instantly said.

"Well, unless the three of you know any of the Feds in the field offices here that you can trust, we have no choice. We have no idea who is in this cartel's back pocket and we can't risk Monroe getting out of the country."

I knew it wasn't going to be that easy. I knew it wasn't the smartest thing in the world to be going in with just us, but we also didn't have many options here. We couldn't use local law enforcement because we couldn't trust them. We had to go at it alone, which meant we needed a plan. A solid plan that would keep us all safe and alive while we went in and grabbed Monroe. The cartel wasn't going to hand him over to us, so we were going to have to take him.

"We're gonna need more weapons," Rafe stated.

"I'll get to work on getting the images," Cooper said, before he went back to his laptop.

I could tell none of them were happy about the situation or the proposed plan, and we were going to need more weapons and gear. That, at least, I could get for us without raising any red flags within the agencies.

We had to do this smart and we needed a solid attack plan.

Tonight, we were raiding the cartel's

stronghold and I was going to be ready for any possible outcome. I wanted Monroe alive, but if we had to, then we'd kill him and end this, once and for all. The investigation into the child trafficking ring he was a part of, or running, would just be started, but that was something we could handle on our own if Monroe died here. The first step to ending all of this, though, was to get inside that stronghold, no matter what.

CHAPTER TWENTY-FOUR

Jarod

I COULDN'T STOP the trembling in my hands, no matter how hard I tried. This day had not been going the way I expected it would. I didn't expect much, but this wasn't exactly it. Walking under the cover of darkness to creep through a forest that led to a cartel's stronghold wasn't exactly on my life's bingo card. I had done raids, but nothing like this. When I had done raids, it was with an extreme amount of cops against a small number. This was six guys going against an army of one hundred, all so we could capture Monroe. It was the next level and intense, and I had no idea if I would ever be good enough for something like this. I didn't have the training that these guys had. I was very much a rookie, here, and I hated that I didn't have anything helpful to offer the team.

I felt a hand on my forearm and I turned to see Mason. We were both partnered up for our takedown position and having him here with me was the only thing keeping me together.

"Relax, it's going to be okay."

He was trying to comfort me and make me feel better, and I appreciated the effort. But I doubted there was anything he could possibly say to me, right now, that would make me feel better.

"This is insane. I'm not good enough for this."

I didn't belong in this situation.

I wasn't trained enough.

I was a liability by being here.

I could get one of them killed because I wasn't good enough.

I had no business being here.

I could feel the panic starting to rise and I knew I had to stop it or I would be having a full blown panic attack in the one place I couldn't have one.

Mason pulled the com off of his ear and did the same to mine before he placed his hands on my biceps as he spoke.

"Listen to me, you *are* good enough for

this. I know you don't have many years on the job, and nothing like this, but you can do this. I wouldn't have you here if I thought otherwise. Baby, I promise you, I'm not going to let anything happen to you. You can do this. I believe in you."

And just like that, the panic was subsiding.

It was ridiculous and it made no sense, but Mason had a way of calming me. Of making me feel like I could do anything. We barely knew each other, but that didn't matter to my body, to my heart. I was still nervous. I still felt like I wouldn't be able to do this, but I did feel better. I did feel like I would be okay, that we would be okay as long as we were together.

"Sorry," I instantly said.

It was not professional for me to be

acting this way. To be reacting to the situation in this manner. My mind knew that. I just needed my body to know it as well.

"Don't be. You have nothing to be sorry for. Everyone gets scared. Everyone gets nervous when doing something like this for the first dozen times. There's even some situations that I go into that I get scared of, and I've been doing this for seven years. It's a perfectly natural reaction. You got nothing to be sorry for."

As if Mason's words weren't calming me down enough, he moved and pressed his lips against mine. It was brief, but it was more than enough for my body to stop trembling.

For my mind to stop racing.

I was ready now.

Mason pulled back and flashed me a

warm smile.

"We gotta get moving," he said.

"I know. I'm ready," I said, with as much confidence that I could muster up.

He gave me a nod and we both put our earpieces back in. We moved as silently as possible toward our designated entry position.

We had to be careful.

Mason had planned for us to breach at different angles so we could get into the stronghold and, hopefully, go as unnoticed as possible. The one thing working in our favor was that Monroe was positioned in the Southern end of the stronghold and he was alone. He had a couple of guards around his room, but that was it. If we could get in as quietly as possible, we had a real chance of getting to Monroe without getting caught.

"Bravo and Charlie, you in position?" Mason asked, referring to the other two teams. Hollingsworth and Cooper were together and Rafe was on his own. Ryzen had been positioned in an Overwatch post further back up on a hill so he could see everything going on.

"Bravo is in position," Hollingsworth said.

"Charlie, in position," Rafe answered.

"Echo, you good?" Mason asked, referring to Ryzen.

"All good, Boss. Clear to breach," Ryzen answered.

"All teams, breach," Mason said, before we both started to move forward.

I followed right behind Mason, keeping close to him to ensure that we wouldn't get separated. I also wanted to make sure I had his back. I wasn't going to allow anything to happen to him.

As we approached our entrance point, he stopped to look at me to make sure I was ready. I gave him a nod and he pulled the door open and we were moving.

We walked into a hallway with our guns raised. I followed right next to Mason as he guided us through the different hallways to reach Monroe's room. We had to duck behind different walls to avoid people, but it was better to avoid them than to have to fire our weapons. That would cause a great deal of noise and everyone would know we were there if they heard gunshots ring out. The last thing we needed was every guard in this stronghold to know that they had company.

"Alpha, target is still in the room with two tangos out front," Ryzen said as we got closer.

"Copy, Echo," Mason whispered.

"We're in position," Rafe said on the other's behalf.

"On my mark," Mason said.

We were both on each side of the hallway by Monroe's room. There were two guards and Mason had decided that him and Rafe would take them out quietly. They had the most training, so it made sense for them to take out the guards. I knew they would be able to do it at the same time and without firing a single shot.

"One, two, three." Mason said, before he was on the move.

I saw him and Rafe come around the corner and grab a guy each in a choke hold. To my amazement, they both snapped their necks, as if they were breaking a paint stir stick.

For some reason, it made Mason look even sexier.

That probably shouldn't be sexy, but I was past the point of caring.

With the guards taken out, we moved onto the room that Monroe was hiding out in. I put my hand on the handle and with a nod from Mason, I pulled the door open and they were storming in with their guns up.

I came up behind them and started to clear the large room. It was bigger than we had expected. Larger than what the blueprints to the stronghold had indicated. The blueprints were out of date and that could become a problem for us.

I had moved to start clearing the area around the window. There was a set up living room and I wanted to make sure he wasn't hiding behind any of the furniture. Though, why he would be, I had no idea, but it had to be cleared.

I had just turned my back from the living area when an arm wrapped around my neck and pulled me back against a hard body. A cold metal against my temple told me that it was a gun.

A gun being held to my head.

A tsunami of fear crashed into me and instantly I felt like I couldn't breathe. I had never had a gun pulled on me, much less held to my head. I must have made a sound, I don't know, because I can't remember, but I must have because instantly, everyone in the room had turned and faced us.

"Put the gun down, Monroe, it's over," Mason barked the order.

Monroe was not going to put the gun

down.

We all knew it.

He wasn't the type of man who was going to toss his hands up in the air and walk away. He was going to shoot his way out of here. And considering I was his shield, I was going to be the last one he killed. I would have to watch Mason get killed and that wasn't something I could handle.

I couldn't lose him, not like this.

"You're gonna let me walk out of here or I'll shoot the piece of shit rookie," Monroe seethed.

"It's over, Monroe. We know what you did. We have witnesses that are going to testify against you. We know you were working with Burn to hide the kids you sold and killed. We found your mass grave. We know everything. Put the gun down," Mason tried.

"You're bluffing. You have no idea what I have done. You have nothing but some hearsay and it means shit here in Mexico. One shot, that's all it will take to alert everyone that you're here. The guards will come storming in here and kill you all."

"He's not bluffing, Monroe. Put the gun down and come in peacefully," I tried, but it only resulted in Monroe tightening his arm around my neck.

"Shut up, you shit. You haven't earned the right to speak," Monroe snarled into my ear.

Before another word could be said, the sound of glass shattering followed by the echo of a gunshot rang out. The pressure around my neck slowly released and Monroe hit the ground with a clear hole in the middle of his head.

I couldn't take my eyes off of him.

I knew I should be moving.

I knew I should be saying something.

That shot didn't come from anyone in the room, so Ryzen had taken the shot.

Ryzen had saved my life, saved all of our lives.

I needed to move, but I couldn't take my eyes off of the freshly dead body at my feet. I had never seen a dead body before. I had never been in a gunfight. I had never gone through anything like this and I had no idea how to process what I was seeing. A hand on my arm snapped my gaze off of Monroe and onto Mason.

"We have to go, now," he said urgently.

I knew the gunshot would be heard. We had to go, or we still risked being killed. Without giving Monroe another look, I ran out of the room after the others and we didn't stop running until we reached the vehicles.

CHAPTER TWENTY-FIVE

Jarod

WALKING INTO OUR hotel room, I could feel my whole body trembling. Now that we were finally safe, my mind was kicking back in. The memories of what just happened were kicking in.

Koda instantly came running at me. We had left him here because we had to be quiet and we didn't want to risk Koda being caught in any of the gunfire, should it go that way.

I moved slowly into the room. I had to get my mind to focus on what was going on, but I just couldn't.

"It's okay," Mason said gently as he came over to me.

He removed my gun and placed it down on the table, along with his. He then turned his attention to the vest I was wearing and pulled it off of me. I knew I should be doing it for myself, but my whole body was shaking. I couldn't control it and there didn't seem to be any way to stop it. I was going into shock or something, I don't know, but I had never felt this way before.

I never wanted to feel this way ever again.

"It's okay. You're okay, Baby," Mason

said, as he pressed a kiss on my cheek.

"I can't stop shaking. What's wrong with me?"

"Nothing is wrong. Your body is reacting to the trauma of what just happened. You've never had a gun pulled on you, much less pointed at your head. You've never seen a person killed before, a dead body. It's a lot and your mind is trying to process it all. You're okay, Baby."

Mason guided me over to the bed and he encouraged me to sit down on it. He quickly helped me to get my boots off before he removed his own. He lifted my legs up onto the bed and coaxed me to lie down before he wrapped his arms around me and I turned into his chest.

"Just breathe. Nice deep and slow breaths. This will pass, I promise."

I knew it would pass, but it felt like it never would, honestly. I had no idea how this could ever be okay again. I trusted Mason, though, and I took some slow and deep breaths to try and calm myself down. I listened to his heartbeat thrumming under my ear and focused on his warm, strong hands moving over my body.

"It's all good. You're safe now, Baby," he said as he placed a kiss on the top of my head, his fingers trailing up and down my back.

I couldn't believe that this whole mess was over.

Monroe was dead.

The kids that we recovered from his house would be safe.

Tyler, would be safe.

The operation was done.

I should be happy, but instead I was sad, because that meant that Mason would be leaving soon for another operation. I would have to say goodbye to him. If this was going to be my last time being held by him, I was going to enjoy it.

I closed my eyes and allowed my body and mind to soak up as much of Mason as I could. If this was the last time I was going to be able to feel him, I wanted to remember even the smallest details.

EPILOGUE

Mason

THIS HAD BEEN a very long case.

It wasn't long compared to some of the cases that I'd had to work. I'd had to chase after a criminal organization for months. I'd had to follow the trail of dead children in their wake to find them and yet, that somehow didn't feel as long as this case had. Maybe it was because of my new PTSD diagnosis, I don't know. I was just glad that this case was finally done.

With Monroe dead, we never had to deal with him again. Tyler was safe and so were Monroe's foster children. Dana had taken a plea deal when the reality kicked in that Monroe wasn't coming back for her. She would be spending the rest of her life in a minimum-security prison. It wasn't what she deserved, but it did end the case, so none of the children or Tyler would have to testify in open court. They could all start to move on and live their lives free from both Monroe and Dana.

The takedown for Monroe was intense, to say the least. I was relieved that all of my guys didn't get hurt. I almost had a heart attack when Monroe put his gun to Jarod's head. I hadn't been certain if leaving Ryzen outside of the compound with his rifle had been the best idea, but I had never been more relieved that I had left him out there. To see the gun held to Jarod's head, to see the fear in his eyes, it ate at my very soul. My whole body had gone cold and I could feel my life being sucked out of me.

I had never felt like that before.

I had never felt anything close to it.

All I wanted was for Jarod to be safe.

It didn't matter what I had to do, I would have given my own life to save him.

Thankfully, Ryzen had been on Overwatch and he was able to make a clean shot. Even still, hearing that shot ring out, I thought my heart was going to stop. I had instantly wrapped my arms around him and pulled him to me. I didn't care what any of the guys thought at that moment.

I had to make sure Jarod was safe.

It was at that moment that I realized how much I had fallen for him.

It made no sense, we hadn't known each other long enough for me to love him, but that was the only emotion I could think of to express the depth of what I felt for him.

It made no sense, but I stopped caring about that a long time ago.

I had learned that what the world dictated as logical could all be forgotten when money was on the table. I had lost count how many times it made sense *not* to sell a child. How many times it made sense *not* to use children to traffic guns or make drugs. But when large sums of money were on the table, all of that logic went right out the window.

So why would my love life be any different?

I was in love with Jarod.

For the first time in my life, I was in love with someone and it terrified the hell out of me. I had no way of knowing what Jarod felt. I had no idea if he even wanted anything to do with me outside of great sex. There were a lot of unknowns, right then, and it was only adding to my stress for the day.

I had a plan for later on today. I was hoping that Jarod would be willing to go with me and that it turned out well. I had no idea what he felt, but I was going to find out today. I couldn't let my uncertainty or fear keep me from not going after what I wanted. Just like I couldn't keep putting my head in the sand and pretending like something wasn't wrong with me.

I had PTSD.

It was time I accepted it so I could do something about it. I was never going to get better, if I didn't start to be honest with myself. I had a lot of work I needed to do, but I was determined to do it. I was being given a second chance with this task force, and I was not about to ruin it.

Walking into the police station back in Gaithersburg had a feel of home to it. I knew it wasn't about the physical station, but rather what the future held. I would be working out of the station with the task force until we were able to secure some funds to have our own station built.

I had to prove to the Governor that the task force was going to work and be highly successful. If I could do that, then we would be able to get a lot more funding and could grow our operation.

First things first, though.

I had to see if I had a team.

The others didn't know that this task force could potentially be a long-term gig, and I was hoping they would be willing to stick around when I asked. We all worked well together and it would be nice to be able to hit the ground running with a team I could trust. If they didn't want to be on the task force permanently, I would have to find more federal agents and start from the beginning again. I really didn't want to go that route.

I wanted *this* team.

The one person that mattered the most to me, though, was Jarod. I was really hoping he would say yes to this. He was a good cop and I knew he had what it took to be a federal agent. The only thing holding him back was his connection to his father, but none of that mattered. He wasn't his father and he didn't deserve to be treated like crap or have to settle because he was afraid of the news getting out.

Working the task force, he wouldn't have to worry about any of that. He would be able to grow his skills and help a lot of children at the same time. It would be great for his career, but it would also be great for me. I would be able to spend a lot more time with him, and that was something I desperately wanted.

The energy in the station was as good as I could expect. They'd had one of their own killed. News of Monroe's death would have spread quickly throughout the station once Captain Perry marked the case as closed.

MASON

The atmosphere was tense, but I expected as much.

They had worked beside this man for the length of their careers. He had thirty years on the job. He had touched a lot of lives and most of them only ever saw the good man he portrayed himself to be. It had been bad enough that we had arrested him, but to hear that he had been killed by one of my guys, it wasn't an easy pill to swallow. It wouldn't matter that he held a gun to Jarod's head, fully prepared to kill him to secure his escape. To most of the cops in this station, losing Jarod to keep Monroe alive would have been the better trade.

To me, though, no one was worth Jarod's life and I would never allow any criminal to take one of my guys. It was just that simple to me.

I headed into the conference room to see my team was already here. Based on the uncomfortable looks and body language, both Jarod and Hollingsworth were not looking forward to being back out in the bullpen. I couldn't blame them. As far as they knew, the Feds were leaving and they would be the ones trapped here to deal with the fallout.

It was just another reason why I was happy to be heading the task force; they would have a different option and they would have backup for when shit got too intense with the local police.

"Thanks for coming in. I know we're all tired and looking to get back home," I started.

"You said it was important," Hollingsworth commented.

"It is important. First, the Governor is

very pleased with our work on this case and how quickly we were able to get it resolved. He would have preferred to take Monroe alive to try and get the location of the kids he sold, however, he knows we were not given a suitable situation for that outcome. He wants you all to know that he is impressed by your work and is proud to have you serving this country."

"I'm just glad we were able to find Monroe and stop him before he could get to any more kids," Cooper said with a soft smile.

"There has been something that I've been keeping from you. I didn't want to bring it up until I knew it would be official. The Governor wants to keep the task force. He's placed me in charge and has given the task force full immunity, with the obvious exceptions. The task force is to go after criminals and criminal organizations that commit crimes against children *Nationwide*. You all have the option of staying with the task force or going back to your original positions. Ideally, I would like for you all to stay. We have something that is working, and I would like to continue working with all of you and grow together. The choice is yours, though."

I was relieved to see the interest in all of their eyes. None of them had a family. They didn't have spouses or a long-time boyfriends or girlfriends. They were all single, and didn't have children. They could easily make a career pivot if it was something that interested them.

I couldn't help but look at Jarod and I was filled with warmth to see the excitement in his eyes. This was something he was very interested in and that meant there was a high chance he was going to say yes. I would be able to spend a lot more time with him and that was something I desperately wanted.

"What exactly would we be doing?" Hollingsworth asked.

"We would be finding cases to take over the investigation for. Then, we would do what we just did. We would find the head of the snake and take them out. We would be going after large organizations like human traffickers, but we would also be going after solo offenders. Anyone that local police haven't been able to find or investigate properly. We could be all over the country at any given day. There would be a lot of traveling and we would have to work with local police, at times, as well as other federal agents. The goal is to save as many children as possible, no matter what we have to do."

"And the immunity, that covers what specifically?" Rafe asked.

"Everything but murder, sexual assaults, and crimes against children. We have a green light for everything else and that does include rough interrogations, should we find it necessary," I answered.

"I'm in," Ryzen simply said.

"Was it the rough interrogation part?" Rafe asked with a smirk.

Ryzen was dangerous, this case had taught us all that. He was a man of few words and he was deadly. He oozed lethal vibes just sitting there. We were lucky to have him on our side, because this man could have easily been on the bad guy's team and that would have resulted in a lot of deaths. Thankfully, he was playing for the good guys' team and he was going to help us save a lot of children while keeping a watchful eye over us.

"Children deserve to be safe," Ryzen simply said, and it was all that he needed to say.

"Well, I'm in. This is important work and I'm not about to pass this opportunity up," Cooper said.

"I'm in as well. Children deserve to have people like us looking for them, fighting for them. I don't got anyone at home waiting for me to get back," Rafe said with a shrug.

"What about you two?" I asked our two detectives.

"Shit, I'm in," Hollingsworth instantly said.

"One hundred percent," Jarod easily agreed.

I couldn't help but be proud of each and every single one of them. They all knew that this was going to be hard, but they were willing to go through any obstacle they had to in order to ensure that children in this country were safer. They were all good men and I couldn't wait until we would be able to take on our next case. We were going to do a lot of good for this country and I was looking forward to it.

It had been a good couple of years since I had felt excited for my job, and it was a feeling I welcomed back into my life.

"Take the week and get yourselves situated down here. There's not much in terms of housing, just yet. My brother has offered his spare bedroom for anyone that needs it. There's also the motel in town."

That was going to be the tricky part,

because in this area, there wasn't much in terms of apartments or houses that went up on the market. I had already decided I would be building my own home. It was going to take some time, but I was fine with that. Roland had told me to live with him, but I wanted my own space, even on the short-term until my house was built. I liked the motel room. It worked for Koda and me. Plus, we traveled so much for work, we didn't need anything more than a motel room, right now.

"I also have a spare bedroom," Jarod offered.

"So do I," Hollingsworth added as well.

"We'll make it work until we can find our own places. If all goes right, we won't be here very long, anyway, with all the traveling. Will we be taking on more people?" Rafe asked.

"When we need them. They don't have to be law enforcement, either. As long as they have the proven skills and take the oath, they'll be fine. We will also be working with two social workers, for now. Isaiah and Travis. We will also need to find a federal prosecutor that we can call up when we need warrants, no matter what city we are in. Roland will be joining the task force as well. Coop, I know you prefer to be in a tech position rather than as a field agent, so with Roland being here, you will be free to stay back in an Overwatch position."

Cooper was an analyst and hacker. He had no interest in being in the field, even though he was trained for it. I knew that, and I appreciated him making an exception with this case. Moving forward, though, I wanted all of my guys to be in their desired position and not to be placed in a situation they weren't comfortable with.

"Thank you," Cooper said with a huge sigh of relief.

"Moving forward, Rafe and Hollingsworth will be partners and Roland will be with Ryzen. Jarod, you will, obviously, be with me."

I knew I could have put Roland with Hollingsworth, but I wanted to try and keep a Fed with a local cop. It would even out the tactical experience throughout the team. Plus, Roland was really good with everybody, so it wouldn't matter if Ryzen said five words a day or not. Roland wouldn't care and he wouldn't feel awkward if there was nothing but silence between them.

"Sounds good. If there's nothing else, I now need to get home and get my house packed up," Rafe said as he stood.

"That's it. I'll see you all in a week," I said flashing them all a warm smile.

Everyone started to gather their things and make their way out of the station. I followed Jarod out, and once we said goodbye to the others, I turned to give him my full attention.

"Wanna go for a drive?" I asked.

"Lead the way," he said with grin.

We made our way over to my truck. Koda jumped into the backseat without any complaints this time. Once we were in, I started to head for the highway. I wanted to take him to the waterfront where we could have a private conversation. I was hoping the sunset background would persuade Jarod to give us a real chance.

I didn't want just a sexual relationship with him.

I wanted a real relationship.

I wanted to go out on dates and learn everything there was about him. I wanted something real. For the first time in my life, I wanted more than just meaningless sex.

I could hear Roland's voice in my head now telling me "I told you so," but I was choosing to ignore it.

I was going to allow myself to be happy.

To have more than just my career in my life.

"How are you feeling about the task force?" I asked as we hit the road.

"I'm excited for it. It sounds like it's going to be a really good thing. I know it will be hard plenty of times, and I'll see things that will make me wish I could bleach my brain, but saving kids, that's something I am willing to risk everything for. What about you, though? It'll make your PTSD worse, won't it?" Jarod asked, concern flooding his voice.

I had been worried that he would look at me differently when I had confided in Jarod about my PTSD diagnosis. I wasn't really sure what he saw in me to begin with. We hadn't known each other that long, still didn't, really, but I didn't want him to see me as weak. I couldn't even begin to explain the relief I felt when that look in his eyes never changed. Still, doing this job would keep aggravating my PTSD and there would be many nights ahead of me that would be hard, but I also knew that by pushing through, I would be saving a lot of innocent children and that would be worth the sleepless nights.

I would have to find a way to balance it all out.

I would need to find a way to cope and live with my PTSD, but I would figure it out.

I was not about to let my PTSD ruin me.

Not now, not ever.

"I'll manage it. I'll start taking it seriously and speak with someone and I'll manage the triggers and stress. It is possible to do this job with PTSD. Plenty of federal agents do it all the time. I will figure it out."

Jarod reached over and placed his hand in mine as he spoke.

"We will. You're not alone in this

battle, Mason."

I turned my hand so ours could intertwine as I spoke.

"I know. What about you? Are you okay with the possibility of your father's identity coming out?"

"If it does, then it does. I'm not going to hide who I am anymore."

"Good. The guys won't care, either. You don't have to worry about that. Just be yourself. That's the best thing you can do."

He gave me a rich smile before he spoke again.

"So where are you kidnapping me to?"

I gave a soft chuckle before I spoke.

"I'll never tell."

"All right, but don't expect me to fight if your cuffs come out."

I couldn't help the groan that escaped

me as the memory came flooding into my mind.

That was a good night, a very good night.

It was a night I was looking forward to experiencing many times over.

***

It was close to an hour later when I parked my truck at the beach. The sun was just starting to set and I knew it couldn't get any more romantic if I tried. Romance was something I was new at and I was going to make a real effort with Jarod. I wanted him to know how special he was. How much I cared about him.

We got out of my truck but I left Koda in the backseat. He wasn't too happy, but I would let him out soon so he could run around and play.

"Wow, this is very romantic," Jarod said as I took his hand and walked him toward the water.

"You deserve romance," I countered.

"You deserve more than sex, even great sex. You deserve dinners, and breakfast in the morning. I know we said this would just be sex and I know what I'm about to say sounds insane. We've barely been around each other and we don't really know each other, but Jarod, I love you. And I don't want just sex with you. I want to build something real with you."

I had no idea what he was going to think or feel about anything I just said. I knew, typically, there would be more time before saying those three little words. We should have spent months having casual sex before admitting that we were in a relationship and then the I love you's would come out. However, in our line of work you weren't guaranteed a tomorrow. You weren't even guaranteed the next hour. I didn't want to waste what precious time we had, not for a single second. I had to make sure he knew how I felt, even if that meant he didn't want the same.

Jarod stopped and turned toward me. I could see the emotion brimming in his eyes and could swear they almost sparkled.

"When I first met you, I felt like I had already known you. It was as if we had met before, but I know we hadn't, because I would have remembered a man like you. It feels as if we knew each other in another life. It makes no sense, but there's a connection there. I feel it every time I'm around you; have from the very first moment I saw you. There's no logical reason for me to feel this way, because it is too soon, but I love you, too, Mason. And I can't think of anything that I want more than to spend as much time with you as possible," Jarod said with his emotions echoing in his voice.

Hearing those words, hearing that it wasn't just me, that he loved me, too, I felt like a little kid on Christmas morning. The pure joy that flooded my entire body, I couldn't even begin to explain it. Words had escaped me, so I did the only thing I could do that would convey the love that I felt for him.

I pulled Jarod in for a passionate kiss, one he instantly responded to and wrapped his arms around my neck.

He loved me, we were in love, and that was all that I needed.

We would face the horrors of this world

together and we would free as many children as we could. That was our mission, and we were going to do it together.

I would face it all with the man that I loved by my side until my last dying breath.

Thank you for reading!

Turn the page for a preview from Rafe, Book 2 in the Federal Protection Agency series.

PREVIEW

Finley

THE WHOLE PLANE was filled with music as we all celebrated another successful mission. I had been in the Navy for six years, now, and I had loved every minute of it. Yes, there had been missions that left me feeling hurt on every level, but this right here was what made it all better. Being around my brothers, feeling their love and our family, this is what made everything worth it. All of the hard hours, the hard labor, the horrible things we had seen, it was all worth it to be able to be a part of this family.

"Excuse me, gentlemen, I have an announcement," our Commander said as he joined us.

The music was turned down and we all gave him our attention. I was hoping that we wouldn't have another operation. I had been looking forward to sleeping in my bed after being out for two months. This operation really had taken a lot longer than we ever expected.

"It is my pleasure and honor to inform all of you that Petty Officer Finley Quinn has just been accepted into BUDS."

I was instantly up on my feet cheering along with the rest of my brothers. I hated that I would have to leave them to become a Navy SEAL, but I would be able to follow in my brother's footsteps and I was beyond excited. I couldn't wait until I could start.

I was instantly attacked by a group hug by my brothers and it was only another reason to celebrate on our way home. As beers were given out, I took mine and headed over to a quieter place on the plane so I could video call John. I had to tell him what happened. After three rings, his face appeared on my phone.

"Hey, Baby Brother, you finally on your way back?"

"About halfway there, now. I just got word... I made it into BUDS. I'm going to be a SEAL, Big Brother," I said, with the biggest smile on my face.

I couldn't believe I had made it. My dreams were coming true and I couldn't contain the excitement that was flowing through my veins. I could tell John was feeling the same when a huge smile split his face.

"Yay! That's my boy. I knew you would. My team is all set for you. The guys can't wait to have you join us."

I couldn't wait to be there.

When I had joined the Navy, John was already a SEAL and had been working with his team for a while at that point. I had been around his team plenty of times when I was younger, and the second I graduated Boot Camp, they were all set for me to come and join them once I had enough experience to qualify for BUDS. I had even joined them on training days and completed different training courses with them to help me get ready for what BUDS would have in store for me. It was going to be insanely hard, but I knew it would be worth it in the end. I would finally get to operate with my big brother and there was nothing I wanted more in this world than that.

"I can't wait, man. Where's my little princess?"

"She's right here. She just finished brushing her teeth for bed."

John moved the phone over and handed it over to the best thing in my entire world. My beautiful niece, Lilly, was just five years old and she was my everything.

I had known I was gay when I was ten years old. I had told John about it when I was twelve and he didn't even bat an eye. He just asked me if there was a boy I liked. Whenever I had a question, he answered. He had done his own research on homosexual relationships and how to give me the 'sex talk.' It never once bothered him and that only made me love him even more. When he told me that him and his wife, Darla, were expecting, I was over the moon. I knew that little baby would be the closest thing I had to a child and I was going to love them with my whole being.

"Uncle Finnie!" Lilly said with the biggest smile her face could make.

"Hello, my Princess. How are you?"

"Good. You come see me?"

"I am. I'm heading back home, right now. Once I get there, I'm going to shower, pack, and then head out to you guys. I'll be there in the morning and I can't wait to see you."

"Tea party?"

"Absolutely. I am packing my best tea party outfit. And do you know who else is excited to see you?"

"Mizzie?" She asked with a bright smile.

I reached over and picked up Mizzie.

Mizzie was Lilly's favorite doll. She was a twelve-inch long mermaid that had long, shiny pink hair and she was well loved. She had given her to me when I went away on this operation for good luck and I knew how much the doll meant to her. She wanted me to have her so I wouldn't get lonely and she would be able to keep me company.

Me and the guys had taken photos with Mizzie while on our operation. She had been all over the base and in the humvees. I had sent all of the photos to

John to show Lilly and she loved it. She had made John print them out so she could hang them up on her wall to show off Mizzie's adventure.

"She is very excited to see you," I said as I showed Mizzie to Lilly.

"I miss her. She come tomorrow?"

"She will be with me and she can't wait to see you and tell you all about her adventure."

"Morning?"

"That's right. We're going to be there right after breakfast, my Little Princess, and I don't have to leave for a whole week. We're gonna have lots of fun together."

I was getting the week off and I couldn't wait to spend every second of it with Lilly. I already had plans to take her to a water park and a petting zoo. I was also going to spoil her with a mini shopping spree at her favorite toy store. It would drive John insane, but I didn't care. She was mine to spoil and I had every intention of doing just that for the next week.

"Okay, Uncle Finnie. Daddy says it's bedtime. I love you."

"I love you, too, my sweet Little Princess, and I will see you in the morning."

She waved goodbye and I said a quick goodbye to John before he ended the call. Tomorrow morning, I would get to hold her and see my brother and sister-in-law. I couldn't wait to be back home with them.

***

It was just before ten in the morning when my cab turned onto John's block. I was a ball of excitement to finally be able to get to hold the two most important people in my life once again. The second we arrived on the block, though, we were at a dead stop.

I looked out of the front windshield and to my horror the street was flooded with cop cars. My blood ran cold and I did the only thing I could do. I handed over some cash for the ride and grabbed my bag. I was out of the cab and running toward my brother's house. The whole time, I kept telling myself they had to be there for another person. They couldn't be here for my brother's house. The closer I got to it, though, the more my dread increased.

The second I saw the yellow crime scene tape, I dropped my duffle bag and ran at top speed toward my brother's house. I ducked under the crime scene tape and ran inside. I didn't care about the cops that were calling out to me or chasing after me.

I had to find my brother.

I had to find Lilly and Darla.

I don't know what I was expecting as I ran into the house, but it looked like it always did. There was no sign of a struggle, no blood. At least, not on the first floor.

I ran up the stairs and headed for my Lilly's room. I had to make sure she was okay. A detective grabbed me right at her door, but it was too late, I had already seen what was waiting for me.

My brother, my hero, my protector, my idol, was there on the floor. Dead. He died right there in that room, multiple gunshot wounds to his back, and I knew without a doubt, he died protecting Lilly. I felt my legs give out, but the arms that were wrapped around me, kept me up.

"No, no, no," I said as I took in the sight of my dead brother.

"Sir, I need to know who you are," the detective said.

I needed to talk. I needed to identify myself so they wouldn't arrest me for trespassing, but I couldn't stop looking at John.

This wasn't supposed to happen.

I was coming home for the week.

We were going to celebrate me getting into BUDS.

I was supposed to be on his SEAL Team and working with him.

We had plans and now all of that went up in flames and for what?

They didn't have much money, the

place didn't look ransacked, so what was the point in any of this?

"Sir, I need your name," the detective demanded as he started to pull me away.

"Finley Quinn. That's my brother," I managed to say as I forced my body to work and take my own weight.

"Mr. Quinn, this is a crime scene. I need you to come outside with me."

"Lilly, where's Lilly?" I asked, urgently, as I pulled away so I could start looking for her.

"Mr. Quinn, you are going to potentially destroy evidence. I need you outside, now. I promise, I'll answer your questions."

The very last thing I wanted to do was ruin any evidence that could put the son of a bitch who killed my brother behind bars. I knew I wasn't going to win an argument with the local cop, either. He could have already arrested me, but he hadn't. I followed him outside and spoke again.

"Where is my niece? Where's his wife, Darla?"

"I'm sorry to be the one to tell you this, but Darla was found dead in the home as well. Your niece isn't here. It looks like she missed out on all of this. Do you know where she was staying last night?"

"No, she was here. I spoke to them around eight on video call. She was just getting ready for bed. They were all home last night."

If Lilly wasn't in the house, that meant whoever broke into their house took her and there was no telling what was happening with her, right now.

"Are you sure she didn't go to a

friend's place this morning?" the detective asked, now worried as well.

"No. I was coming down on leave for a week. They all knew I was going to be here this morning. Lilly was going to make a tea party. She wouldn't be anywhere but the house."

"Okay, I'm going to put out a BOLO. Do you have a recent photo you could send me?"

I just gave a nod and pulled out my phone, doing my best not to let my hands shake. I sent him a few photos that I had gotten just last night from John as I spoke.

"John, he's a Navy SEAL. You need to call NCIS. This could be connected to something he was doing for the Navy."

"I'll reach out to them once I get the BOLO up. Did either your brother or his wife tell you anything recently about any threats? Anyone that maybe had been causing them problems?"

"No, nothing like that. Darla, she's a stay-at-home mom. John, he works for SEAL Team Eight. I can send you his teammates names and contact information, they might know more."

"I would appreciate that. What about Lilly? Have they mentioned any new friends, anyone that maybe had been around a lot, an adult at the park without kids?"

"No, no, if someone was hanging around John would have handled it. They don't have any hired help. The front door is always locked and the alarm is set. Lilly doesn't go over to anyone's house, not even for play dates, they all happen out in public. Even at birthday parties, either

Darla or John attends with her. John was paranoid with Lilly. We both were from our job. She was always protected. Her window even has a security bar on it so it can't be open more than five inches."

I wished I had someone I could point the finger at. I would have gone over to their place and beat the truth out of them. My niece, my world, she was out there somewhere and I had to find her. I wasn't going to stop until I did.

"Okay, please, don't go anywhere. I'm going to need to talk to you more. I'm going to get the BOLO out, now."

I just gave a nod and looked toward the house as the Coroner went inside.

This wasn't supposed to happen.

This was something that only happened to other people, this didn't happen to us.

They were good people, they were safe and now they were both dead and Lilly was out there somewhere.

She had to be terrified.

I had to find her.

I turned my attention to my phone and started to call the guys on John's team. I was going to have an army out on these streets looking for Lilly and none of us were going to rest until we found her.

Snag your copy of Rafe at your favorite online retailer!

OTHER BOOKS BY EVIE

Federal Protection Agency
Mason
Rafe
Ryzen
Cooper
Noah
Damien
Sebastian
Gabe
Logan

Ruthless Empire
Courting Danger
Chasing Danger
Kissing Danger

Smokejumpers
Hawke
Cyrus
Jase
Gage
Jackson
Xavier

ABOUT THE AUTHOR

Evie Riley is a prolific, neurodivergent author known for her captivating MM romance novels. She has gained a significant following and topped the LGBT+ action and adventure bestseller charts with her series.

Evie's writing style often explores dark and gritty themes where her men must overcome difficult obstacles in their search for love, but she has also ventured into sweeter small-town romances, incorporating tropes like enemies-to-lovers, friends-to-lovers, age-gap, and forced proximity. She is known for crafting engaging romantic suspense novels and has a knack for creating interconnected series worlds that keep readers invested.

Interestingly, Ms. Riley has hinted at exploring new genres, such as Alien Omegaverse Romance, in the future.

Outside of writing, she enjoys spending time at the beach and has a quirky personality, described by her partner as ranging from cute to deadly, depending on her blood-chocolate levels.

Evie spends her nights writing bad boys in love, and her days wrangling the sweet boys she loves.

~Evie Riley

www.ingramcontent.com/pod-product-compliance
Lightning Source LLC
Chambersburg PA
CBHW061051210726
48294CB00001B/94